# CHASING VALENTINO

## A HOLLYWOOD BY THE SEA NOVEL

### JULIE CAROBINI

DOLPHIN GATE BOOKS

# ALSO BY JULIE CAROBINI

### Sea Glass Inn Novels

Walking on Sea Glass (book 1)

Runaway Tide (book 2)

Windswept (book 3)

Beneath a Billion Stars (book 4)

### Otter Bay Novels

Sweet Waters (book 1)

A Shore Thing (book 2)

Fade to Blue (book 3)

The Otter Bay Novel Collection (books 1-3)

### The Chocolate Series

Chocolate Beach (book 1)

Truffles by the Sea (book 2)

Mocha Sunrise (book 3)

### Cottage Grove Cozy Mysteries

The Christmas Thief (book 1)

The Christmas Killer (book 2)

The Christmas Heist (book 3)

Cottage Grove Mysteries (books 1-3)

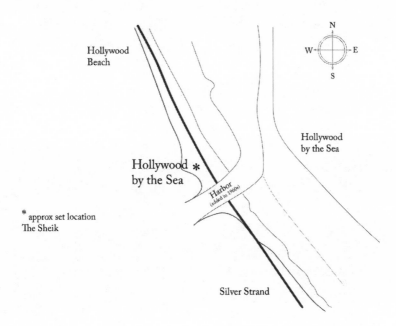

Hollywood
Beach

N
W   E
S

Hollywood
by the Sea

Hollywood   *
by the Sea

Harbor
(added in 1960s)

* approx set location
The Sheik

Silver Strand

*To my paternal grandparents,*
*Gabriel & Maria Navarro,*
*who rubbed elbows with the stars back in the day*

# CHAPTER ONE

**GRETA**

SOME PEOPLE WERE DISTRACTED by shiny things, but I'd never been one of them. I preferred the stable and true, the promise of a life overflowing with goodness, fidelity, and love. To some, those *were* the shiny things, but I disagreed, because shine doesn't last. Over time, it tarnished and needed some good old-fashioned elbow grease to buff it out so it could shine again. The love I'd been looking for would be like that, though I had yet to come close.

I was willing to wait because when it came, it would be real. And that's all I'd ever wanted.

Frankly, for a time, it's what I believed I had found.

My breath caught as I stepped outside on a blustery late spring day and opened the mailbox. I thumbed my way through the stack of mail. Ads mostly. A bill or two. No pastel envelopes. The tension in my shoulders relaxed some. So far, nothing related to the wedding that would never be.

A rustle of discomfort brushed against my face, the wind still too cool outside, though it was late spring. It should be warmer by now in Indiana. As if by habit, I rubbed that empty space on my ring finger.

He had been perfect for me. Everyone had said so. And for a while, I had convinced myself that Tommy was exactly what I needed—*who* I needed—for the rest of my life. The realization of our wedding date looming still, mere weeks away, chilled me to my toes.

I stepped inside the house again, thankful for the warmth embracing me.

"Any big checks in there for us?" My sister, Clara, who shared the house with me, often said that. Usually her quip lightened the mood, but this time, not so much.

"Nothing." Thankful for no more congratulatory cards or gifts that had to be returned, I plunked the stack of mail onto the kitchen counter. As I did, a thin postcard slipped out. I frowned and picked it up, holding it to the light. "What is this? It looks ancient."

Clara stepped closer, looking over my shoulder. "What ... is that a one-cent stamp?"

I ran my fingers across the stamp with George Washington's picture on it. "Feels real. But who ...?" My words stopped when I saw who the postcard was addressed to: Lizzie Pomeroy.

"That last name ... it's so familiar," I said. "Look at the postmark."

Clara gasped. "That was—" she counted on her fingers —"nearly a hundred years ago! What in the world does it say?"

All the drama that had been on my mind dissipated. I gathered a breath and read:

. . .

Dear Lizzie,

Time has passed, and I wanted you to know how much you are dearly missed. Do you miss me too? Have you found what you were looking for?

Well, as they say, the grass is always greener on the other side. I do hope, dear Lizzie, that you have found this to be true. Of course, if this is not the case, you may always come back to me.

In the end, I fear you will find that you have made the right choice. I only wish I had as well.

I looked into my sister's eyes. "It's signed, 'R.'"

"But who's Lizzie?"

"Lizzie ... Pomeroy." The thought jolted me. "Could this be for Elizabeth Pomeroy? Our great-grandmother?"

Clara looked as if she might faint, but she revived enough to lunge toward the card again. "If so, this is incredible. I wonder who 'R' is. Well, *was*." She continued to marvel at the card, her gaze glued to it. "Greta, this is the craziest thing I've seen come through the mail. Do you think it's real?"

"The handwriting is faint, but there's a smear of ink at the top, as if written by hand. Doesn't look like it was printed, like an ad might be."

Clara shook her head slowly. "What's on the other side?"

I flipped it over to find a photo of a large arch standing in sand with the words *Welcome to Hollywood by the Sea* emblazoned across it. I bit the inside of my lip, while sliding a look at my sister. "Florida, maybe?"

Clara shook her head. "No, it's in California."

"Really." I continued to hold the card in mid-air, as if the light would somehow provide an x-ray to the past. "How do you know?"

"I remember Grams telling me about it one day." Clara reached up and touched the card as if doing so made it that more real. "I didn't realize it was this place until right now. Anyway, when she was doing better, she mentioned that there was a place by the coast in California that actors used to call Hollywood by the Sea."

"Actors, as in, starlets? Like our great-gran?"

Clara nodded. "I believe this was the place Grams mentioned. She said that her mom, our great-gran, lived there for a time. I guess they used to make movies there."

"Good memory."

Clara shrugged. "What can I say? It's the writer in me."

"So many questions." I let out a sigh. "Questions that we will never have answered, I suppose."

Clara gently took the postcard from my hand. "Unless you go there, maybe. To find answers, I mean."

"Where? California?" I forced a laugh through the cloud that hung over me, chasing my cheeriness away.

"Why not?" Clara's face lit up. "You certainly have the time."

An unfortunate truth. For years, I had saved up enough vacation time from my event planning career to sail away on the honeymoon of my dreams. When Tommy proposed, I saved even more. Then during one bitter cold day a few weeks ago, my boss, Jan, delivered the suffocating news: She'd sold the company and signed a non-compete clause. Not only would Jan be moving on, but I would have to as well.

"Unfortunately," Jan said, "the new owners will not be retaining any of our staff."

I was washed up by thirty-two.

Clara continued talking, as if I had not been weathering my share of blows lately. "So anyway, if I had money in the bank like you, I'd do it in a heartbeat."

I wagged my head. "Oh you would not."

"Well, fine, I probably wouldn't." She laughed heartily. "You know the introverted me too well. But you ... *you* love meeting new people, so I'll clarify: If I had your savings and your extroverted nature, I'd get on a plane tomorrow."

"I wouldn't call myself an extrovert."

"Oh no? You tell all the grocery clerks your life story when all they ask is how you're doing! It's so embarrassing."

"You're ridiculous." Her crazy talk brought a smile to my face for the first time all morning. And, for half a second, I considered Clara's idea of traveling alone on a quest, even though she surely said it in jest.

If I were honest with myself, I would have to admit that since my engagement to Tommy ended, I had entertained more than one brief thought of flying off to ... well, anywhere but here. I bit back a sigh. It didn't help that everywhere I went in this small town, reminders of him—of *us*—seemed to crop up. Still, the thought of flying away always died quickly, like an ember landing on the frosty, hard ground of winter.

I shook my head while pulling a glass from the cupboard. I filled it with water and turned, leaning my behind against the kitchen counter while taking a drink. A sigh escaped me as my reality continued to sink in. "I appreciate the wild thought, oh creative one. I really do. But the best thing for me to do is keep myself busy. We both know I'll get over this sooner or later."

"Of course you will. I may be the fiction writer of the family, but you're the true romantic. Hopelessly romantic, actually. You'll probably find your true prince before I finish my next outline!"

"Ha ha ha. Right. Good try."

Clara's voice softened. "I hate seeing you this way. Maybe you should start your own business. You always have been more of a leader than a follower. You could try, you know."

Truthfully, I hated acting this way, too, let alone feeling like a grumpy, sad sack of a woman. Wasn't like me. But the risk of starting my own business scared me. I didn't have the confidence to see it through—I should know that by now.

Clara was right about something else, though. I *had* grown up on romance novels, the squeaky-clean kind that promised true love that lasted forever. I'd latched onto them as true-to-life scenarios—even though neither Clara nor I had seen that play out in our lives, what with father leaving when we were kids and our grandfather dying before either of us was born. We only knew of our great-grandparents through snippets passed down.

Admittedly, I lapped up Grams's sometimes vague recollections of her father. He sounded kind and generous and true to our great-gran. Always. But how true was what we had heard?

As I'd grown older, I'd begun to question those memories —it was natural for that to happen, I would say. Maybe our sweet grandmother preferred to remember her parents as devoted, when actually, only one of them was. Same with my grandfather. And father.

In the end, I decided that our grandmother's stories sounded, well, just too good to be true.

I reached for the postcard again, gazing at it for a good long time. "You are something, aren't you? Where've you been hiding?"

"Do you think the post office noticed the postmark?"

"No idea. Good thing we live in Great-gran's house or we may never have gotten to see this treasure."

We were startled by the ring of the doorbell, followed by the distinct sound of a truck starting up.

"I'll get it." Clara headed for the door.

Mesmerized by the postcard, I examined it more closely and continued to wonder who "R" from long ago might have been. The sound of Clara re-entering the house caught my attention.

My sister crept closer, a sullen expression marring her face and a rectangular package in her hands.

"What is it?"

Clara swallowed. "It's addressed to you. And Tommy."

Oh, for heaven's sake. For a long few seconds, I couldn't speak. Shew. I was much too young to feel this old, but honestly, navigating life's burdens had become so tiresome lately. How would I ever move on if nobody would let me?

"Sorry to be the messenger." Clara turned the large padded envelope over. "Wedding gift, maybe?"

I groaned. "I just can't ..."

Clara looked expectantly toward the package.

"Fine. Go ahead and look."

Clara tore open the envelope and slid out a canvas-covered frame. She winced.

"What?"

"It's the engagement photo of the two of you. It says in fancy letters that your household was established, um, this year."

I sputtered. "But I'm sure we told everybody the wedding was off. Who sent it?"

Clara turned the envelope upside down and shook it. Nothing came out. She glanced at the front of it, frowning. "There's no return address. No card."

"What in the ...? Let me see." I reached for the package and thoroughly inspected it. It had not come via the post office. There did not appear to be any postmark or any other way to figure out who had sent it.

I slapped the empty package down onto the table. "Great."

"I'm sure whoever sent it meant well," Clara said. "They probably ordered it a while ago and forgot about it."

"I suppose."

I forced myself to look at the gift fully now. To the untrained eye, it appeared as if Tommy had surprised me with the ring. But really, I knew he was going to propose. He'd dropped enough hints about my clothes and my nails that I knew to be prepared. And I was. My clothes were new, and I'd had my nails done that very morning. In reality, the spontaneous event was meticulously planned.

But we'd been happy then, right? Both of us? For a brief second, I closed my eyes, wishing to barricade myself against the sudden onslaught of memories. Clara stood close by me, and yet, I felt so very alone with my second guessing and unsaid fears.

*In the end, I fear you will find that you have made the right choice. I only wish I had as well.*

My eyes snapped open at the memory of those words, a not-so-sudden thought prodding me along. I reached for the postcard that had, by some kind of miracle, reached us all these years after it had been sent.

The penmanship put today's texting to shame. The sender had written with a kind of deliberation and thoughtfulness absent from today. And in an instant, I knew.

Clara eyed me. "What's going on in that head of yours?"

"I've made a decision." A fire stoked inside of me. "I'm going to go out of town for a little while—to Hollywood by the Sea."

---

DEAREST MOTHER,

I HAVE ARRIVED. I hope Father is not still angry with my decision. It is beautiful here. The people are fine, and being in California is all I have ever wanted. I know already this to be true.

Please do not worry. I will write more soon.

LIZZIE

# CHAPTER TWO

**GRETA**

Two PLANES, one long layover, and a sticky hour-plus ride from the airport and I'd made it. I stood in front of the narrow house on the California coast, suitcase leaning against my shin. This trip had occupied my thoughts for weeks—ever since my moment of epiphany back home. And now? I had nothing but sand, sea, and sleuthing to occupy my time.

Case in point: I'd already learned that Hollywood by the Sea was nearby, but that my rental was part of an area known as Hollywood Beach. Already, there was much to learn.

I pressed my lips together briefly, unsettled by how much I still missed Tommy. Especially now when I was far from home on what should have been the best day of my life. How was that for divine planning?

Oh, I was over it. But when my car wouldn't start and

Clara was asleep and I had to find another way to the airport, I almost told Siri to call his cellphone. He was still in my Favorites.

More than once I'd picked up the phone to tell him about the new suspicion that I shared with my sister last week. It had come to me like a lightning flash in the night, so I did a little research. When I'd first told Clara of my surprise findings, she gave me that subtle eye roll of hers.

"Seriously, Greta, maybe you should be the novelist in the family," she'd said. "That's some creative scenario you are envisioning."

"I don't know why it hadn't occurred to me before."

"That our great-grandmother once had a torrid love affair with the actor Rudolph Valentino?"

"I never said torrid."

She scoffed then. "If that had been the case, I think we'd have known about it."

"Maybe, maybe not." I strained to recall the scant stories, like confetti from butterfly wings, that our grandmother had told us, with our mom goading her on in the background. Times like this made me wish I had paid more attention to them both. Maybe then the spattering of words would somehow make sense now. Mom had been gone for years, and Grams? These days, especially, her recollections didn't always add up.

I shook my head, bringing myself to the present. Whatever the outcome, I'd traveled here to wrestle with the questions. That, and to forget about the future I'd once planned to have with Tommy. Truthfully, he would have never let me take things this far. He saw life in black and white. Not a bad thing, especially when making decisions. But for me, life always seemed to play out in hues of the color of sky and dreams.

That soft early summer breeze blew strands of hair around my face. I needed to move on. The loss of my engagement to Tommy was more than the simple disappointment of seeing an event cancelled, like one might feel about a meeting whose speaker could no longer attend, or a picnic that had been suddenly rained out.

The heaviness of it all still weighed down deep in my bones. But my tears had been spent, and I had experienced a reckoning. If the only reason to marry Tommy was to have a person one phone call away to rescue me from the annoyance-du-jour, then the breakup was for the best. I had to believe that.

A shredded flag with a half-naked mermaid on it whipped in the breeze. There were no sidewalks here. Just miles of neat houses lined up and craning for their own slim view of the sea. The house was two stories, gray, with a not-so shiny red door. A few shingles were missing—okay, more than a few—and frankly, it could use a good washing with a high-power hose. Still, it would do, and I was happy to have found this place to stay on such short notice. The owner occupied the first floor and rented a lock-out upstairs to vacationers. He had told me by email to help myself to the key.

A lockbox swung from the front door handle, but I still didn't feel quite ready to go inside. Instead, my mind took a snapshot of the quintessential beach house, faults and all, waiting to beckon me inside because, well, it reminded me of why I had really come so far.

"You really think there's a possibility that the 'R' in that postcard was the famous actor?" Clara had asked again last night before I'd left the kitchen to settle into a fitful few hours of sleep.

"I have no idea," I answered, drying the last pot. "But maybe walking where she walked—"

"And where *he* walked," Clara interjected.

"Yes. Where they both walked ... well, maybe I can at least quell my questions."

"Such as?"

I didn't answer her right away because the romantic in me wanted to know why our great-gran would choose to walk away from it all. Instead, I said, "Oh, you know, like what it was like to live in California and make movies around the turn of the century. Things like that."

"Wouldn't mind knowing about that time too," she'd said.

Clara and I had spent weeks trying to piece together those stories we had heard about our great-grandmother's days as a movie starlet and how that could play into the contents of the postcard. We even approached Grams, who lived in an assisted living home, but she clammed up as if holding onto a pearl.

We had become so very used to that.

In the end, the timing was prophetic. I hadn't wanted to admit it, but I had become bored. With no wedding to plan, complacent. Surely, the suffocating doldrums would flit away now. Wouldn't they?

The closer the time came for me to leave, however, the more Clara fretted.

"I thought you wanted me to go," I said, one evening. "Aren't you the one who thought it would be fabulous to find out how Great-gran once lived?"

"I guess."

Clara had been born with a suspicious mind, something I

never really had. She'd half-accused me of agreeing to marry
Tommy to get away from her. "If you don't want to be my
roomie anymore, Greta, just say so."

When I had told her the marriage was off, she showed
the appropriate amount of sympathy, followed by unmasked
delight.

But as the day loomed for me to leave, Clara could barely
hide her disappointment.

"You know, you're going to be fine here," I assured her.
"I'll only be gone for a few months."

"You say that now, but you'll probably take one look at
that gorgeous blue ocean and decide to move out there
forever."

"So dramatic you are."

Her pout was pronounced. "While it's true that I
encouraged this trip, a week away should have been suffi-
cient. Why do you have to go for so long?"

That *was* the million-dollar question, wasn't it? Truthfully, I wasn't all that sure of the answer.

Clara continued her mini-rant. "I just want to point out
once again that, well, you're an extrovert."

I laughed. "This again."

"Greta, you'll wither and die if you don't have any
friends to hang out with all summer while you're gone."

"I'll make some."

"But you won't have me—your favorite sister."

"I'll always have you. If you're lonely, call one of our
cousins. Might have to reintroduce yourself, you know, since
it's been so long."

Clara's sigh was more pronounced this time. "They all
have their own lives. I only have"—she looked around—"my

computer. And even he shuts down sometimes when I'm talking."

"You mean *it*."

"It what?"

Your computer is an it, not a he."

Clara dropped onto the couch. "See? Even my relationship with my computer is short-circuited."

I laughed, glad to see how well she was taking this.

That distinct right eyebrow of Clara's rose. "So you're saying you won't worry about me."

I dropped into a comfortable wing chair, the one we had argued over at the big box store but eventually settled on anyway, and faced Clara. "Look at me, sis. You will be okay. More than okay without me around. I promise."

Clara screwed up her mouth. "Easy for you to say. I'm an introvert working from home. You leave and, well, I'll have to get a cat."

"At least that means you'll be leaving the house for longer than it takes to get the mail. You know, since you'll need to pick up cat food."

"I'm not that bad."

"Then come with me?"

"All the way to California? Um, that would be a no. Indiana would miss me. So would this house ... my bed."

"And your cat."

A layer of uneasiness rumbled beneath the surface of our laughter. After a while, when a hum of quiet landed between us, Clara looked up and speared me with a look that I've yet to shake.

"Don't abandon me," she said.

The words very nearly caused me to cancel my plane reservation and unpack. My wild plans to travel to the area our great-grandmother had once walked suddenly felt silly. Shallow. Futile.

As I wrestled with that decision, I smoothed my thumb across the surface of the old postcard, once again marveling at the neat handwriting that had withstood the years. Truly remarkable.

My eyes alighted on my sister's. "I have to go—but I promise you this: I will never abandon you. Ever."

And now, days later, here I stood, rooted on the street, gazing at the beat-up house I would call home for three months. Sisterly concerns aside, it had taken quite a bit of rearranging for me to get here, what with preparing files to hand over to Jupiter Events, the firm that bought my former company.

I had actually run out of time. Even the clothes in my suitcase needed laundering—something I wouldn't ever share with anyone.

My eyes took in the condition of the sparse garden in front of the rental house. Weeds overtook the planters. Lavender blooms under the canopy of palm trees needed deadheading. And quite frankly, the entire mess could use some water and thick soil to cool its roots. What were left of them.

I sighed, hearing my sister's voice in my head: *Why should you care about all that when you're on vacation?*

With a quick shake of my head, I grasped the handle of my suitcase and began making my way toward the short rise of steps. Unfortunately, those insufferable weeds still called out. My grip tightened on the handle. I repeated to myself— *I'm not here to spruce up the planters.* Or to do laundry, really. *Quit being so OCD.* I shook off the overwhelming desire to drop to the ground and start yanking those dry old weeds right out of that bed and, instead, made my way to the front door where the rusty lockbox swung from a handle.

"Well, dear Great-gran," I whispered, "let's see what kind of secret life you may have led." A few quick clicks and I stepped inside.

---

DEAREST MOTHER,

I AM safe and learning to enjoy the ocean. I am very careful! The movie set looks like a desert, with piles of sand everywhere, though the ocean is but a short walk away.

While the other girls and I waited for our time on set yesterday, we walked to the shore and dipped our toes into the water. It felt like ice and soon my feet throbbed from the cold. It was a small price for us to pay because later we saw a dolphin, the most magnificent creature I have ever beheld!

I dare say I could live here forever.

LIZZIE

# CHAPTER THREE

**ZAC**

AT LEAST THE results were benign. This time.

I logged off my computer, thankful for the break after working right through lunch. I knew I had it easy. I spent my days interpreting medical findings that, depending on the results, could make someone's life a whole lot better. Or ten times worse. The best part for me was that I rarely ever had to tell anyone bad news to their face. Made avoidance easy. Never liked talking all that much anyway. Freed up my time to work on a million other projects crowding my brain.

I reached overhead, grasped my wrist, and stretched back far enough to remind myself that I'd been sitting at this desk, in this darkened room of my home, for far too long. I'd been at the lab until late last night and had decided to plow through my reports from the home office.

My phone sat off to the side of my desk in Do Not Disturb mode, but my eyes caught sight of the screen showing that someone had left a message. A scowl found its way to my face, dragging my mood down with it.

I debated whether to listen to my voice mail. For the first time in my eight-year career as a pathologist, I had never— not once—been called to defend myself like I had recently. Dread attempted to overcome me again, but I pushed it off. I wasn't one to shy away. Avoid, maybe, but run away? Never.

I picked up the phone, found my voice mail and deflated. Wasn't the hospital. It was Lisa. She had left two messages.

I groaned and ran a hand across my stubbled face. Would there never be a day when I could put the lousy years behind me?

A whine at my feet spurred action. The dog I had inherited—or kidnapped if Lisa was to be believed—headbutted my leg, no doubt needing to pee. "Hey, Sport."

She whined again, and I detected a protest in her glance.

"That's your new name, girl," I said. "Better get used to it."

I grabbed her leash, and she barked. Then she spun around like some kind of obsessed animal, her nails tap dancing across my hardwood floors. *Add that to the list of bad behaviors I needed to train out of her.*

Outside, Sport led the way down the block, squatting twice, first at a light post and next near a shrub, probably to show her euphoria over this midday romp. My eyes adjusted to the light as my head simultaneously ran through the list of tests that needed interpreting by the end of day.

"You've got that look on your face, Zac. Gonna call the cops again?"

The sound of the woman's gravelly voice gave her away —my neighbor Helen. She walked toward me, pushing her husband, Gus, in his wheelchair.

I stopped, despite Sport's insistent tug on her leash. "Good morning. How are you both doing?"

"Lousy," Helen said. "My knees creak when I walk, and the sound of the foghorn kept me up all night."

I gave her a bemused smile. "I'm sorry to hear that, and surprised, as well. That foghorn has the opposite effect on me. It actually helps me sleep."

"She's talking about me," Gus piped up. "I told her to put some cotton in her ears, but will she listen?"

A lightbulb flipped on in my head. "Ah. I see."

"Forget about him." Helen wagged her chin. "You need to get out more. Go stick those toes of yours in the sand, young man—before your knees hurt too bad to walk across that beach!"

Gus butted in. "Tell 'im what you said to me this morning."

"Eh?"

"I said tell Zac what you said to me this morning, over breakfast." When she didn't respond right away Gus grunted and slapped the air with his hand. "Forget it. I'll tell him myself." He lifted his chin. "Said you don't get out enough. Thinks you need a woman."

My head was crammed full of information, data, unfinished projects, and keeping my head above the surface of all of it. One thing I had no plans to pursue anytime soon was a woman. Far from it. It had been months since Lisa ended our engagement, and I'd finally come to the realization that it was for the best. My mind had never been clearer about that.

Sport tugged at her leash, reminding me of her formidable presence and need for a walk. Can't say I was all that unhappy about Lisa leaving her dog behind. I'd stopped answering her calls after she tried to ship Sport off to a friend of hers. When that didn't work, she wanted her sister to take her. I wouldn't have it. If she wasn't willing to care for the dog herself, then she had no say left in the matter. Lisa had managed to upend my world and then wiped my life clean of all that we had shared together. Wasn't about to give up the mangy beast too.

Sport barked once, indicating she was ready to go.

"Oh, you hush now." Helen frowned at the dog before lifting her chin in that *what-for* way of hers. "You think I'm old and don't know nothin', but I know plenty. And you, my dear, have been down in the mouth for too long."

Gus nodded. "Yeah, buck up, man. Someday you might be in one of these contraptions"—he slapped the armrest of his wheelchair—"so find yourself a young one to push it for you."

Helen slapped him on the top of his head. Gus didn't flinch.

I took that as my cue to let Sport take the lead, offering up the old couple a wave and the best smile I could muster. I didn't mind occasionally running into them on my walks, but they could be tiresome.

Have to admit, though—maybe Helen was right. Not about finding a woman—I would not be traveling down that perilous road again for the foreseeable future. But the getting out part. A man could only converse with a computer screen so long before he began to lose all social skills. I knew this deep down, no matter how hard I tried to disregard it.

*Go stick those toes of yours in the sand, young man— before your knees hurt too bad to walk across that beach!*

Despite myself and the looming predicament regarding my career, a lightness emerged. I slipped out of my shoes and began to walk down the coastal access between two old cottages that faced each other, both of them remains from a bygone era that would probably be torn down soon.

Yes, a walk on the sand was exactly what I needed, with a dog—and only a dog—as my companion. That was enough for me. And, I suspected, would be for a very long time.

---

**Greta**

THE INTERIOR of the house was sparse, not to mention narrow. Tidy, in muted gray tones. Not the beachy kind with pops of blue, either. The living room was outfitted more like an office than a home. Except for the white leather couches that flanked the gas fireplace in the middle of the room—a surprising touch in a room full of layered grays.

Maybe the lack of homeyness was because the owner was male. His terse emails almost made me search for another place to rent, but there was nothing else in my price range. Or frankly, quite so close to the beach and in such good condition. Well, sort of.

I accepted his terms of a rather large security deposit and a promise not to bring a dog, a party, or excessive noise to his happy place by the sea.

Not that he called it that.

He hadn't even replied after I, in a moment of gut-wrenching honesty, thanked him for accepting my reservation and telling him that I would be traveling here on what was supposed to be my wedding day.

Cringeworthy. Truly.

Ignoring my rising inner turmoil, I looked around.

Surprisingly, this place had great lack of ... kitsch. So far, I didn't spot one *Life is good at the beach* sign or a pillow with a mermaid on it or even some kind of *Gone fishin'* shadow box. I thought I remembered spotting a mermaid sculpture in the pictures of this vacation rental listing, but maybe I had imagined it.

Instead, some of the walls were blank. Lackluster. While others wore small framed prints of nautical themes. A weathered sailboat. The wheel of a ship. An old sea salt with a pipe hanging from his creased lips.

My phone buzzed in my pocket. I resisted the urge to look at the screen. Tommy had probably discovered that I had disabled the GPS app that once made it so easy for us to find one another. Was he calling to say he had noticed?

"It's for your own good," he'd told me.

So I'd let him punch in my code—he already knew it anyway—download the app, and accept his request on my behalf. He joked that now he would be able to find me anytime, anywhere.

I admit now that agreeing to sign up for that app and give Tommy access to my whereabouts sometimes made me feel akin to a dog on a lead. I'm sure he never meant for me to feel that way. Now that our relationship was over, I hope he understood why I had deactivated the account. Maybe he wished he had thought of it first.

I turned off the phone and hurried into the bedroom to unpack. The small closet was plenty big for my needs, with hangers and cubicles for folded items. The small shoe rack made me pause. I'd brought my old running shoes with me on a whim. Tommy thought women who ran looked gaunt, so he'd encouraged me to take up cycling with him. I enjoyed it, though hated having to dodge traffic in tight spaces. But the truth was, cycling never gave me the endorphins running once had. It had been so long since I had put on running shoes and headed out on foot, that I couldn't exactly remember why I loved endorphins in the first place.

With a shrug, I plopped my running shoes onto the rack, then I threw on a pair of shorts and a T-shirt. Both needed laundering, which made me gag a little, but I pushed on. I pulled my long hair into a ponytail and covered it with a baseball cap. But before I turned to leave, my eyes landed on my open suitcase. A copy of Great-gran's postcard—Clara made me leave the original at home—stuck out of an interior side pocket.

I plucked it out and re-read the last couple of lines for—how many times was this?—hundreds. Or at the very least, dozens.

"You made the right choice. I wish I had."
                - R

I STOOD THERE A MOMENT, contemplating, before leaning the postcard up against a nightstand lamp. Shoes changed now, I grabbed a garbage bag and stepped outside to the haze of the day.

The air felt different this time of year from where I lived in a little town not far from Fort Wayne. The air at home felt crisp, not weighted by the salt and moisture surrounding me here.

A brief search turned up a small bucket and trowel in the shade along the side of the house. Quite a bit of rust on it. A quick rap of my knuckles on the owner's door downstairs proved fruitless, so I dropped the bucket near the flower bed and went to work. I wasn't a gardener, per se, but did like to keep the land around our little home trimmed well and planted up. The effort and sweat always made me feel as if I'd done something worthy.

I breathed in another lung-full of that air. Weeding didn't feel quite so laborious with the distant cry of seagulls and that warm salt-air breeze for company. Spring came early in California, unlike home when it could fake you out one day and go back into hibernation the next. The thought flittered through my head that I could get used to this, but then Clara's face appeared in my mind. She wore a frown.

A deep voice interrupted my musings. "It's about time."

I wrenched a look up, shading my eyes with one hand. "Excuse me."

The man had a diamond-shaped face, dark scruff with a hint of gold, and when he removed his sunglasses, I could see eyes as blue as the Pacific Ocean.

"The garden's been overgrown for months." He gave the front door of the house a quick, sobering glance. "I said it was about time the owner hired someone to make it look decent."

"Oh. Yes. Uh-huh."

Those well-shaped lips of his curled downward. "I suppose you're getting the place ready for another crowd."

"A crowd? I don't understand what you mean."

He shrugged, and the dog at his side began to prance. "This place has a reputation for its revolving door of vacationers. Can be tiresome."

"I suppose it could." I threw out my standard response to someone who I believed was being irrational, but I didn't want to say so. But then—and I don't know why this happened—in the silence between us I became suddenly very honest. "Not everyone can afford to live at the beach."

He appeared startled by my response, and his gaze began to travel down my length, getting caught up on the rip in my T-shirt. I wanted to call him out for that. I also wanted to change my shirt.

He nodded once, then, as if my words had gotten to him. Instead: "Sounds like you're saying the pretty boy should pay you more. I'm not surprised he's lowballed you."

I shook my head.

"Don't try and defend him."

I stabbed the dirt with the trowel. "Listen—"

The front door swung open, and a guy with perfectly still blond hair, dark sunglasses, and leather slides stepped out onto the stoop. "Mornin' neighbor," he said to the man I found myself in a debate with. "I see you've met my new tenant."

The intruder frowned at the picture-perfect man on the front stoop—my vacation rental host, apparently. The neighbor then swung his gaze back at me. "You might have mentioned that."

I narrowed my eyes at him, while also aware that my Midwest manners were on the line. "And you might have introduced yourself before assessing my attire and concluding that I was the gardener."

He eyed me, a tickle of a smile on his lips.

My landlord continued on, his voice smooth as Italian espresso. "You keep this up, Zachary, and the poor woman will think Californians have no manners." He lowered his shades, his eyes meeting mine. "Poor Greta came all the way here to get over a broken heart. The deadbeat up and left her at the altar—or something like that." He replaced his shades. "Broke my heart to learn of it."

Zachary frowned. "If that were possible."

I looked from one antagonist to the other. I really needed to learn that while a word spoken might flit off into oblivion, email was forever. I didn't need my landlord telling my secrets to a stranger.

I thought about slinking off, but something about the way the neighbor eyed me clawed my insides, reminiscent of the way Tommy always thought he knew what was best.

Abruptly, I extended my hand to him. "Greta," I said, simply.

"My apologies, Greta. I'm Zac." He tilted his head toward the house with the SUV. "Neighbor."

"Hm."

One of his brows rose. "I meant you no harm."

"And yet you assumed I was the gardener."

"Nothing to be ashamed of."

"Still, weird." No sooner had I said the words when Zac's little dog bounded over to me, rose onto her hind legs, and planted her paws on my thighs. Despite the awkward meeting, I laughed and massaged her ears while looking into her plaintive eyes. "You think he's weird too, don't you, sweetheart."

Zac whistled, attempting to coax the dog away from me, but she wasn't budging.

I lifted the tag hanging from her collar and raised a questioning eye in his direction. "Bubbles?"

My landlord pulled his glasses all the way off his face this time, revealing a stunning smile. "Bubbles, eh?"

"That's an old tag." Zac whistled again. "C'mon, Sport. C'mon, girl."

"Hm, I don't know." The dog continued to paw me, her pink tongue hanging from her mouth. I gave her a good noggin rubbing. "She's responding much better to Bubbles."

My landlord laughed more heartily this time, and I caught his eye, a second of solidarity rising between us. "You are Carter Blue, I presume?"

"I am."

Carter turned his attention back to Zac and continued to laugh, more openly now "Bubbles is quite the name for a dog. Could you not think of anything more cutesy?"

"You mean, something like Mermaid Manor?" Zac folded his arms across his chest, still hanging onto the leash. "Oh and by the way, is weeding the garden part of your rental agreement now?"

I batted at a stray hair that had slipped out of my hat, tucked it over my ear, and glanced at my temporary landlord. "I hope you aren't offended that I took this upon myself, Carter. Gardening relaxes me." I didn't mention that seeing weeds every time I passed by would have needled my last nerve. Even to me that sounded ridiculous.

"Don't mind him." Carter pushed out his bottom lip as he spoke to me but stared at Zac. "He and I have had our ... differences. You go on ahead and garden all you'd like. I have an array of tools in the shed out back, and you are welcome to help yourself."

Zac looked directly at her. "And when you're done with that, you can paint the house and fix some of the loose shingles too."

Carter smirked. "If we're done here, I have clients to attend to." He turned away but stopped abruptly. "And Greta, welcome to Hollywood Beach. I would love to share more about the area with you, so let's plan on a glass of wine on the balcony sometime soon."

Zac and I watched Carter pull his Mercedes out of the garage and take off down the narrow street. When he'd gone, I looked over my shoulder, hoping Zac had gone. He hadn't.

I turned more fully to him now and tilted my head to the side. "You enjoy being a jerk, don't you?" I'd never said that sort of thing to a stranger, not ever.

"It was a joke."

"Maybe try a different profession." I pulled the trowel out of the dirt. "Comedy isn't your thing."

He stood there in the quiet, staring at me, as his dog gave up and sprawled flat against a sunny area of the driveway. Struggle shadowed his eyes, but I couldn't muster any sympathy for him. Still, I was tired and in an awkward situation. And I hadn't come all the way here to make enemies on my very first day.

A rueful thought crept into my mind. If this were one of Clara's novels, she'd find some way to turn the situation into a love triangle. What a nightmare that would be. Thankfully, I wasn't in the market for a man. Just a vacation to hunt for clarity of Great-gran's past.

Zac whistled, and his dog leaped up and shook her hairy little body from head to tail, like she was shaking the sun from her fur. "Perhaps I'll see you around. Goodbye, Greta."

"Maybe so." I paused and winked at his dog. "And bye to you, too, Miss Bubbles."

Wordlessly, Zac turned on his heel and left.

---

Dearest Mother,

. . .

THE AIR CAN BE QUITE cold here, even in summer. Sometimes when we are filming, the wind picks up and I have to smile as if sand has not already made its way between my teeth! These are small inconveniences for such excitement.

Oh, Mother you will be so happy to know that I have made friends with Mary, Anna-Rose, and Margaret. Every one of us believes we will find our way out of small roles and into stardom.

Please tell Father I am being very careful not to converse with men alone. (Do not mention that part of my work means I must be in scenes with many males sometimes.) Even Mr. Valentino appeared today!


LIZZIE

# CHAPTER FOUR

**ZAC**

WELL, that went well.

I slammed my keys onto the counter, marched to the refrigerator, and opened the door. Empty except for a single IPA, an apple, and some kind of cheese. Or was that salami? The perils of long days at the hospital.

I shut the door again and stood upright, running a hand through my hair. What had just happened?

The last hour had been nothing special nor out of the ordinary. A break during another tiring marathon of work. Get up. Walk the dog. Breathe some air. Back to work.

Should have been easy. I rubbed my hand across my face, aware of the grizzle, and stopped. I had made a fool of myself in front of that ... stranger. I glanced upward. *Lord, why did I open my big mouth to that pretty boy's tenant?* I groaned. There was no answer forthcoming. The woman had looked at me as if I were mad. And a jerk.

Maybe I was both.

As if the dog sensed my ever-darkening mood, Sport aka *Bubbles* trotted over and rubbed her side against my leg. Traitor. All I wanted to do was go for a walk. Get outside and suck up some oxygen. Clear my head of blood samples, tissue, and random bodily fluids. Instead, I was accosted by a stranger.

Or had I accosted her?

The woman carrying a bucket and shears continued to stay on my mind as if a hole had been bored into my skull and the unlikely encounter dropped inside. That ball cap on her head, those denim shorts that fit her body well, and that holey T-shirt that had obviously tumbled around in someone's dryer far too many times continued to play across the dark screen of my mind.

My hand landed on the kitchen counter. "You're losing it."

Sport whined. It sounded like Scooby Doo, so I shot her a look. "I'm allowed to speak out loud in my own home."

She looked unimpressed.

My phone buzzed in my pocket, and I managed to shove aside the goings on of the past hour to read my email. Duty called, and I'd never been one to shirk that. Quickly, I scrolled through my messages and stopped at a subject line:


Zac, we need to have a discussion. Call me.

I STARED AT THE WORDS, my mind kicking into work mode, trying to decipher the hidden meaning, like it was a tissue sample holding a secret.

It was no use. I needed to hear the decision straight from the boss. I pulled up his phone number and hit the call button.

A SABBATICAL.

The word wasn't in my vocabulary. It certainly had not been in my mind when I returned the boss's abrupt call.

"You haven't taken a vacation in three years, Zac," Dr. Perez had said. "It's time."

"I'll consider it, Doctor." Truthfully, I doubted that I would. "But I'm in the middle of several descriptive reports that I must get to this week."

"Make them summaries. That's all anyone reads." He paused before adding, "Most of yours are usually too long anyway."

Too long? His words were like a blow to my sternum. I tried to protest, but in his characteristic, somewhat long-winded way, he would not allow it.

"This is not a suggestion, Zac." Dr. Perez had released a weary sigh into the phone. "You're the best we have, but even the best must take time out for reflection and respite. As a doctor, I'm quite sure you know the health benefits of time away from an overburdened work schedule. Get yourself outside. See people, not just stool samples."

Silence.

"Or is it possible," Dr. Perez said, "that your longtime

absence from the floor has caused you to forget what it's like to be among the living?"

My mind slammed with myriad arguments, but I knew when I'd been beaten. That last statement, in particular, had smacked me in the gut. When given the option, I had willfully chosen less time on the hospital floor and more in the lab. In the end, I accepted my fate and hung up the phone.

I stood in front of my desk, both grief and relief churning my insides. Sport scratched her fur against me, like she'd suddenly become feline. I glanced down at her. "Buckle up, Sport. Looks like you're gonna be seeing a lot more of me around here."

I had hoped for a distraction from thinking about my meeting with the girl next door—not to mention the mud I'd managed to get on my face at the same time—but not this. Unbelievable. With a twist of my lips, I wandered into the guest room that had been converted to a workroom and surveyed the mess in there. Parts—wire, screws, bolts—all over the place, sketches, an open tool chest.

For a brief second, I laughed. Lisa would take one look at the disarray and go nuts. She would flip that wild blonde mane of hers over one shoulder, punch her fist into her waist, and tell me that it all "had to go."

In the days leading up to our marriage—the one that never materialized—had I not acquiesced to her demands and housed my projects in the garage? I surveyed the room again while Sport danced around my feet. Having everything within sight would be so much better.

I closed the door to the room, as if the mess would magically disappear. Mess or no mess, there was little chance my ideas would ever completely shut off. Staring into a computer screen, I'd learned, made my brain crave creativity.

Though my colleagues would find this difficult to imagine, I often conjured up project ideas while in the midst of preparing a very technical report. Not that I would ever have much time to execute them all.

My sigh billowed in the silence. Too much of my life had been wrapped around Lisa—and work—for this new reality to feel natural. I eased myself back in front of the computer, but for once, couldn't focus. My mind tumbled backwards over thoughts I hadn't much considered lately—reminisces of the past, memories thought buried.

Before Lisa, there was Mary. She hooked me with brown eyes and her great love of cooking. When she cooked, she smiled. There was no untangling of the two. Truth be told, I thought she was *the one*, though I would never have used such a cliché to describe our relationship. But with her, I *had* expected a future of red wine, soft lips, and a never-ending supply of homemade tamales every time I walked through the door.

A small smile reached me, followed by a sickly note of dread.

Mary left me faster than a street taco in the hands of a hungry teenager. I expected to forget about women for a while, but then I met Lisa while waiting for my car to be washed. Of all places. She upended my stiff upper lip—her words—with a game she had made up to make the time pass faster: match the car with its owner.

Lisa straight up told me that she had a near perfect record and that she could prove it. Of course, I let her. I remembered watching her, eyes determined, tongue stuck to her upper lip, as she only missed one call—a purple VW bug driven by a guy with tats on the back of his head. I sat out in front of that noisy car wash as Lisa entertained me during the wait with her rapid-fire speech and distinct laugh. That and the fact that she matched me up with my SUV perfectly.

After my killer heartbreak with Mary, I was ready for someone like Lisa, a person who seemed to know me, maybe even better than I knew myself. And all signs pointed toward Lisa wanting the same for herself. I did everything I thought she wanted: proposed, bought the beach house she had her eye on, and kept myself busy working and remodeling the place while she planned our life.

But it wasn't enough.

First, Mary.

Then, Lisa.

I hung my head, feeling the twist of my mouth, like I had bitten into a rotten apple. Two broken relationships with one common denominator: Me.

I sucked in a breath, noting the blink of my computer screen. One swipe of my mouse would reveal that never-ending list of scans that needed my attention before the day was through. And when that was done, I was not quite sure what I would do. I glanced out the window, noticing the newcomer walking across the street toward the beach, her shoes hanging from her fingers.

Sport continued to snore quietly by my feet, and for the moment, all seemed peaceful in my home. Why would I want to do anything to mess all that up? I took a seat at my desk and got back to work, eager to avoid any distraction by the temporary girl next door.

---

DEAREST MOTHER,

. . .

EVERY DAY they tell us not to speak on set so that the actors can think, but you know how very difficult that is for me. I have so much to say! As I write these words, a smile finds my face. I am reminded of your strong voice. In my mind, I can hear you say to me, "Elizabeth, if you need to speak so often, go to your room and pray to God the Father!" I am trying to remember to do that, though I have no room of my own now.

Stay assured that I am careful to listen to the director and follow my cues. Oh, Mother, it is much harder than it looks. One step off our cue and the scene will have to be filmed again!

Please tell me Father is no longer cross. I am still quite happy.


LIZZIE

# CHAPTER FIVE

**GRETA**

I GLANCED at the clock on my nightstand, my eyes not fully open. At home, I would dawdle some, then drag myself into the kitchen in search of caffeine. Then again, it would be three hours later there.

I pulled myself up, determined to get my body clock on board with my new surroundings. Despite the lack of warmth in this place, Carter had thought of everything a short-term renter needed. Last night I washed and dried my clothes, grateful he left detergent in the laundry room. I'd have to thank him for that.

Dressed in soft sweats and a hoodie now, I stepped outside to the morning sun making its way across the sky. Never thought of myself as a morning person, but somehow, the beach was drawing that lifestyle right out of me.

The road was narrow, with skyscraper-style homes along my walk, yet the sea roared too loudly to miss. Although it had been a hundred years or so since my great-grandmother walked along these shores, somehow I hadn't expected it to look so ... modern.

I stepped to the side to allow a car to pass. In the distance, an old couple—one in a wheelchair—straddled the middle of the road, and I hoped they, too, would hear the car coming upon them.

I continued on, my mind replaying that strange interaction with Carter's neighbor yesterday. Such a shame. Zac was a handsome guy, and under other circumstances, I would have looked twice. And probably lingered on that second peek. The twinkle in his gaze made me think he was joking at first. And though he claimed he was, it hadn't felt like it. Heat emanated from him, and not in a good way.

I pushed thoughts of him away and realized I'd come upon two old cottages with a clearing between them. Could these have been here when Great-gran once was?

Unlike the many mini-mansions lining the coastal block that faced the sea, one of the cottages was built perpendicular to the street. Or, at least, perpendicular to the current street. Its garage faced north, unlike the more common east-facing layout. Who knew what had been in the mind of the builder so long ago? Or how the area may have looked?

I took in the other cottage, its clay-tile roof and warm-toned stucco, smoothly applied. It wore simple lines that held up against more complicated dwellings nearby. The house looked serene and oddly quintessential against its backdrop of soft sand and glimmering water. I could almost hear it release a sigh in the tangy breeze.

I sensed I had company and noticed the older couple approaching. The old man, who sat in a wheelchair, pointed his cane in the direction of the cottages. "Those old houses have been here since the 1920s."

His caregiver scrunched up her face. "She doesn't care about all that, Gus. Do you, hon?"

I smiled. She must be his wife. "Actually, I'm very interested."

The woman hooted a laugh. "Oh now you've done it. He'll talk your ear off if you let him." She shook her head. "I only hope my knees can hold up long enough."

"They filmed a movie here called *The Sheik*. Bet you didn't know that."

Actually, I did. But I only smiled. "Do you know where they filmed it?"

"Sure do." He craned his neck to look up at his wife. "Turn this thing around, will you?"

Dutifully, she did, but not without allowing me to see her eyes rolling.

He poked his cane to the south, toward the harbor. "Was a big ranch that way, full of dunes. With all those mountains of sand, it looked just like the Sahara Desert at the time."

"So you think the movie was filmed where the harbor is now?"

"About right. Or a little to the north of it. They made other movies there too."

"You seem to know a lot about it."

The woman cut in. "He's nearly old enough to remember when all that really happened." She laughed heartily.

Her husband gave her a playfully dangerous frown. "She thinks I'm an old codger, but I don't care. Never was much for fiction, but I love facts. And this place has all kinds of interesting ones."

I was beginning to think so too. I smiled at him and extended my hand. "My name is Greta."

His eyes lit up. "Like Garbo."

I laughed. "Yes. And my sister's name is Clara."

He pulled his chin back, almost as if wondering whether I was teasing.

"It really is," I said.

"Like Bow? Clara Bow?"

"Yes. My mom was a fan of the twenties."

His wife slapped one of the push handles. "Well, I'll be. She actually does know what you're talking about, old man."

"I'm Gus, and the old lady's my wife."

She nodded. "Helen."

"Well, Gus and Helen, I'm happy to meet you both."

Helen winced, but quickly followed with a curious smile. "Do you live around here, dear?"

"No, but I'm staying in a vacation rental for the summer. I only arrived yesterday, so this is my first walk in your beautiful area."

Gus nodded. "If you ever want to know more, I've got all kinds of stories for you."

"Some of them true!" Helen said.

A breeze kicked up, and Gus pulled the blanket up further on his lap. The sun shone, though it was barely sixty degrees. Perfect temperature for me, but I dutifully zipped up my hoodie. "It was a pleasure to meet you both. I really do hope we run into each other more."

A car approached from the distance, so we said our goodbyes, but before she'd walked two steps, Helen cried out, more than a wince appearing on her face.

"You all right back there?" Gus asked.

I stepped up and reached for the push handles. "May I?"

"Yes, oh, please do." As I took control of the wheelchair, Helen leaned up against me. "Sharp pain in my knee. Always happens when it's cold."

Gus harrumphed. "I told you it was too cold to go out."

"No, you didn't!"

At the groan of an approaching car, I almost suggested that she sit on Gus's lap for the ride home. But how would they take that?

The vehicle stopped beside us, and Zac was behind the wheel. "Is there a problem here?"

Helen released a sigh. "Zachary, you're my hero."

Now it was my turn for an eye roll. I controlled it, though.

"Hello, neighbor."

I greeted him with a quick nod.

"Helen," he said, "can I give you a ride to the house?"

"Oh, but I don't know."

She casted a fretful look my way, but I nodded my head and waved her on. "I can take it from here. No problem."

Zac put the car in park, opened the door, and hopped out. With care, he helped the old woman walk toward the car, but when he began to open the back door, Helen protested. "I don't get to sit up front?"

My gaze met his briefly, but I looked away, only hearing their conversation.

"Of course, you can. Would you like me to carry you around to the other side?"

I hadn't expected that. Apparently, neither had Helen because her gravelly voice softened into butter. I sneaked a peek as she patted him on the shoulder. "You're a good man, but I can walk if you'll let me lean on you."

Gus and I watched as Helen shuffled to the passenger

seat, clinging to Zac's arm. When she was in her seat and Zac had returned to the driver's side, Gus looked up at me. "She has the hots for him."

I nearly snorted.

As they drove away, Gus tapped the ground with his cane and pointed it northward. "You push, and I'll regale you with stories on the way."

I laughed and followed his guidance. As I pushed Gus down the street, he did indeed tell me stories while pointing out houses here and there, some new, some old, some he did not approve of. "Ruins the ambience of this place," he said more than once. "This place used to be crawling with Hollywood types. Charlie Chaplin, Douglas Fairbanks, even Clark Gable! Lots of 'em came up for vacation."

I was about to ask Gus what else he knew about those years from times gone by when he tapped the ground with his cane. "We're here."

"Here?" I slowed.

When he nodded, a strange sort of realization, like puzzle pieces fitting together, came over me. We were standing in front of the house next to my rental, and Zac's SUV was in the drive. How had I not noticed him turn in here?

"Go on now. I'm getting overheated in this thing."

I startled. "Of course." Wheeling him up the drive, I noticed the small sign with a number and an arrow pointing toward a path on the side of the house.

"We have the bottom floor, in case you're wondering." Gus craned a look at me. "Zachary lives upstairs."

A short wooden ramp had been secured to the single step up to the unit's front door. Helen called out from a lumpy but comfortable-looking brown sectional in the middle of the room. "Don't mind the mess, Greta! My cleaning lady hasn't been working lately."

Gus winked. "She's talkin' about herself."

I smiled. Thankfully, Zac was nowhere around, which meant I wouldn't have to make chitchat with him two days in a row.

"Can I get you anything, Helen, before I go?"

Gus snorted. "Don't go offering her things. Next thing you know, she'll have you cookin' our supper!"

I cut a look at him but could see the teasing gleam directed toward his wife.

Helen waved a hand. "Don't mind him. I'm better already, but if you wouldn't mind giving the chili a stir in that crockpot over there, I would be grateful. Oh, and on your way back, could you hand me my water bottle?"

"I would be happy to." I dashed into the kitchen, the rich aroma of tomatoes and spices greeting me, although I also detected another spice—sugar maybe?—that I couldn't fully make out.

After stirring the chili, I grabbed Helen's water bottle, my mind slowing as the framed pictures and art on the walls caught my attention on the way back into the living room. Lots of black-and-white memorabilia—a photo of sunbathers in swimwear that covered more than it left to the imagination, an aerial shot, a signed photo of someone from another era. I hesitated in front of the photograph, touched up so much that it resembled a painting. The signature read: *Dear Gus: See you at the beach! Clark.*

"Wow." I leaned in to take a closer look. "What a treasure."

"That one's legit," Gus said.

"Hogwash!" Helen was laughing now. "He got it at some antique show at the harbor."

Gus sniffed. "Well, he may have been signing it for some other Gus, but that's Clark Gable's signature. Mark my words!"

The honest, good-natured banter took hold in my heart. I hadn't seen that emotion coming, and in the most natural way I began to believe that the Lord had led me right to these dear people. And bonus—that Gus might be able to help me figure out where my great-grandmother lived and worked all those years ago.

I smiled at the couple—my new friends—and realized something else: my sister's prediction, the one that I'd go crazy without people to talk to, was correct. Thankfully, I no longer had that to worry about.

I handed Helen her water. "You're much too young to know who Clark Gable was," she said. "Though I suppose you've heard of *Gone with the Wind*."

"Yes, of course."

She pursed her lips a moment. "And you did say your mama named you after famous ladies of the silver screen."

I nodded, my heart taking in all that my eyes could see. For some reason, I felt safe with them. "Can I tell you a little secret?"

They both leaned forward.

"Recently an old postcard was delivered to my home. Well, the home I share with my sister. The card was nearly one hundred years old."

"Well, I'll be," Gus said.

"That's some delay," Helen said. "Postal service ain't what it used to be, that's for sure."

I laughed. "It gets better: The card was addressed to my great-grandmother, who once owned the house. She passed away before I was born, but my grandmother used to tell Clara and me that her mom was an actress for a time in California."

"Let me guess," Gus said. "The postcard read: Wish you were here." He dissolved into laughter while slamming the point of his cane into the floor.

I smiled. "Not exactly. It, well, the writer said that he, um, missed her. That she'd made her choice. Things like that. It was all very cryptic, at least to us."

Gus gave me a grim smile. "A fella doesn't get over unreturned love too easily."

Helen whipped a look at her husband. "What do you know about that? I've known you all your life."

"Except for my years in the service, my dear."

Helen narrowed her eyes at him. "What's her name? You had better fess up right now or there will be no chili for you tonight!"

He chuckled. "Well, if you must know, it's ... Helen." He pointed that cane right at her. "You very well know that you have only ever been the one for me."

"That's right, you knucklehead." Helen gave him a scolding look. "Hush now. Greta was telling us her story."

"That's right," Gus said. "Do you have any idea who wrote the postcard?"

"Sadly, no," I said. I wasn't ready to divulge my suspicion. "We'll probably never really know the person's identity for sure."

"That's too bad." Gus looked thoughtful. "Will you be visiting Hollywood while you're here?"

"Probably not. I don't have a car, although I could rent

one. But the reason I decided to come to this area is that I'd always heard my great-gran had lived here for a time."

"When she was in the movie business?"

"Yes. She was an extra in *The Sheik*."

Helen's face lit. "Oh my word! You hear that, Gus? We have the descendant of a famous actress in our midst!"

"And to think she's spending time now with the likes of us."

I was giggling now. "Gus, I would love to hear more about Hollywood by the Sea's history, if you don't mind a million questions."

"Mind? I would love it, young lady."

We talked a few minutes longer, making loose plans to see each other again. Before I left, I promised I would bring the postcard over soon for them to see, then I gave the chili another stir and headed toward the door. "You sure you're going to be able to get around tonight, Helen?"

She waved me away. "Oh, of course. I'm almost as good as new."

"Okay, then. But if your knee is hurting tomorrow, I'd be happy to take Gus out for a spin in the neighborhood again."

"Hear that honey?" Gus said. "Our beautiful neighbor wants to walk me. Who needs a dog!"

I laughed and shook my head. "That's not what I meant at all."

Helen cackled. "Don't mind him! Old geezer wouldn't miss the chance to spend time talking the ear off a pretty woman!"

"You two." I turned to leave when the exit darkened. Zac had one foot in the doorway and one out. He stuck his hand in the front pocket of his jeans. "You're still here."

"I am."

Indecision crossed his face. He began to turn away, as if he'd suddenly made a decision to leave, until Helen's voice rang out from her perch. "Coming to collect the rent?"

Was that a scowl on his mug?

He caught Greta's eye, then shifted a look inside the house. "No, Helen, not at all. Actually, I have to leave now, but, well ..."

"Sorry, son," Gus said, the tone of his voice noticeably subdued. "I'm waiting for the bank to send me some new checks. As soon as those show up, I will have the rent to you on the double!"

Rent? He was their landlord? Inwardly, I shook away the sense that something wasn't right, my sudden euphoria evaporating as quickly as it had arrived.

But was this any of my business? Probably not. To my surprise, I found myself quickly becoming attached to the sweet old couple I barely knew and was in danger of butting in where I had not been invited. I turned to leave when Helen called out.

"When this bum knee is better, I insist on making you dinner, Greta. You come too, Zachary!"

He gave me an awkward smile, which I returned. When I didn't respond right away, she hollered out, "I'm not kidding! Gus will entertain you with movie trivia too."

Zac raised an eyebrow, his voice low. "Movie trivia?"

I opened my mouth to explain but stopped. I didn't owe him any explanation at all. Instead, I leaned back in through the doorway. "I will look forward to that. See you both soon."

Quickly, I left, only to sense I wasn't alone. A tap came on my shoulder. "We didn't start off on the best of terms," Zac was saying. "And I'd like to offer you an olive branch."

"That's not really necessary."

"Actually, it is. Not only because of my terrible manners yesterday, but"—he glanced back at the open door to Helen and Gus's apartment—"because it sounds like we're going to be seeing a lot more of each other in the next few days."

I shifted my stance and peered up at him. "Why would you think that?"

There was an embarrassed downturn in his gaze before returning to face me. "I overheard you making plans with Gus and Helen. And, well, I've decided to finally do some major renos in there."

"Renos?"

"Renovations. I, uh, have been hoping to get to some things for a while now and after one more day of the grind, my schedule will be clear enough to attack those projects."

"I see."

"So ... I apologize for my quick—"

"Temper?"

"I was going to say assumptions, both about who you were and about the type of renter you would be."

I could feel tension marring my forehead. "What in the world does that mean?"

"I—I ... hold on. That didn't come out the way I meant it." He sucked in a breath. "What I meant to say is that Carter hasn't been known to rent to quiet types who have a desire to be good neighbors. I'm sorry that I didn't recognize you right away as being one of those."

He looked so befuddled and tripped over his apology so much that I couldn't help but let a small laugh escape. "Well, okay, then."

"Does that mean you are accepting my apology?"

My eyes caught on weeds, the ones popping up through the dirt at the edge of Zac's property. I pulled my gaze from them and stared at him a good, long time. "Yes, sure," I said. "I accept."

---

DEAREST MOTHER,

TODAY WAS A MAGICAL DAY! Mr. Valentino brought the most decadent chocolates from Italy for the movie cast. He offered me one. I did not think it wise to add to my figure, but he insisted. I chose to be gracious, like you taught me, and oh, I have never tasted anything so sweet.

I did not have any work today on set after all, but I lingered, hoping to learn everything there is to know about the movie business.

The assistant director, Mr. Winston, is nice to the cast. It is his job to inform the extra actors and to also help stage our scenes, which is a very serious process. He must understand how to frame the scene under Mr. Melford's direction. He asked the cinematographer to let me look through the camera lens. It was very exciting!

I believe every actor and actress should look through the camera lens too. I believe they would see what is important, and what is not.

Please say hello to Father.

LIZZIE

# CHAPTER SIX

## Zac

After I left Helen and Gus's apartment, I tried to decipher the reports on my desk, the ones I had to finish and send off by tonight. For some reason, my concentration had gone the way of bloodletting. I glanced at the clock. Hardly any time had passed at all. Odd. How often had I worked late into the night, the growl of my stomach the only indication that I had worked far longer than was considered acceptable?

So much for finishing well before my so-called vacation started.

I rubbed my eyes with my fists and pushed away from my desk. Sport lay sprawled on the couch in my office. Lisa had bought that piece of furniture on a whim one day, even before the room was ready. Said our beach house would be filled with so many of her relatives and friends that we should shoehorn in one more guest room. Never mind the one she had already outfitted with five-star hotel furnishings

—the cost of the drapes alone had rendered me speechless. And despite all the extra nooks in this place, she insisted on a plush pull-out couch for my office.

Even as I moved about the room, grabbing a sweatshirt, Sport showed no sign of budging. She didn't move one paw.

*Fine.*

Outside, the air was much too warm for the sweatshirt. I crossed the street, pulled it off over my head, tucked it under one arm, and wandered into the market and deli around the corner from the harbor. My stomach grumbled at the spicy aroma of hot pastrami, so much that I could see it in my mind, piled high on rye.

Maybe this was what I needed: a walk, some food. Medical training had long ago made the connection between muscle movement and the brain. I remembered making a promise to myself then, during those long hours of residency, that I would always take time to exercise, to use my legs for more than hustling from patient to patient.

I was thinking about how very long ago that was—ten years? more?—when I recognized the woman standing at the counter in front of me. Could she stand the sight of me twice in one day?

I almost hadn't seen her standing there, waiting for her food while holding a bag of groceries. This woman, who I had not known existed until yesterday, seemed to be everywhere since. Doubly odd considering I hardly went out.

Greta pivoted faster than I could react, and when her eyes connected with mine, it wasn't exactly a smile she wore on her face. So much for our truce.

"Following me?" she asked.

"It appears so."

"Hm."

In the short time since we'd met, she'd made that comment several times. A brief, but dubious "hm." Made me want to give her the third-degree, to uncover what it was about me that she seemed to dismiss with that small tilt of her head and that purr of her voice.

"Or maybe you've been reading my mind," I said instead.

"Highly unlikely."

"Oh really? Why's that?"

"For one, I don't know you well enough to want to read your mind."

"Fair enough. What else?" I hoped she wouldn't bring up the issues I had already apologized for, but given my experience with women, I wouldn't rule it out ...

"What do you mean, what else?'"

"You said, for one, which implies you have further points to make on the subject." She didn't answer right away. Had I gone too far? I didn't have to keep the conversation going. It would have been simple enough to order my sandwich and duck into the market to wait. Pretty sure I could use some new razors. Maybe some dishwasher detergent too ...

"As you know, I'm on ... vacation." She gave up a small shrug. "I'm not here to overthink but to, um, discover new experiences."

I hid the wince that tried to emerge. Now I felt like a dolt. Hadn't Carter said she had just gone through a broken engagement? If anyone knew what that felt like ... well. I caught eyes with her again, this time trying to inject something that looked like empathy. "Yes, of course. How silly of me to tease you when you should be out enjoying yourself."

She quirked a funny little smile at me this time and glanced up at the top of my head again. When she turned to retrieve her food, I peered into the mirrored sandwich case.

My hair stood electrified, as if I'd gelled it into a faux hawk. Nice. I patted it down with my hand and stopped. She was staring at me.

"Did your nap make you hungry?"

"Nap?"

"You know," she said, glancing up at my hair again, "because of the bedhead."

"I haven't had a nap during the day in years." I nodded toward the sweatshirt folded up under my arm. "Guess I pulled this thing off too fast."

"Hm."

I narrowed my eyes at her, but all she did was lift her pastrami on rye in front of my nose. "This sandwich is giant. I can't eat this much. Want half?"

No. I wanted a whole one to devour for myself. But Greta intrigued me. Earlier she'd given off a vibe that she didn't like me all that much, though she had accepted my offer of a truce. Plus, I wanted to know why she had come here, of all places, to nurse a broken heart. Especially since I'd never really wanted to live here in the first place.

She stepped back. "Guess not. Enjoy your lunch—"

"I'd love to take half of that sandwich off your hands," I said, stopping her. "If you really don't want it."

"I really don't want it."

I nodded. "Want to grab a bench? I'll buy us some waters."

She hesitated and realization flooded me. She was giving me her sandwich—not planning to actually eat it with me. But then she surprised me with a "Sure," and quickly walked away and grabbed a table outside, not far from where the gulls waited for remnants.

I followed behind a minute later, water bottles in hand.

In between bites, I sneaked looks at her. Early thirties, probably. Pretty, inquisitive eyes. Button nose. And a curious half-circle scar near the top corner of her lip.

"Why are you staring?"

And she was bold.

I finished my bite. "Apologies. Tell me about your vacation plans. I suppose you picked this spot because it's in the middle between LA and Santa Barbara so you can see the sights. What's on your agenda?"

She slowed down her chewing, her eyes pushed together by a frown. Yes, she was definitely frowning.

Finally, she said, "I'm here to learn about this area. I don't really have plans to go anywhere else."

This surprised me. Why would a single woman from Indiana come all this way just to stay ... here? "Okay. But surely you'd like to see Los Angeles before you leave. Grauman's Chinese Theater? Hollywood Walk of Fame?"

She shrugged. "Not really. I've only been here a day and already I feel like I've just scratched the surface of this beach town. I'd rather see where my walks take me."

We ate in silence, and I kicked myself. She's trying to hide away. Of all people, I should have been able to see that, because I, too, wished I could forget about the past few years. The promises made and broken, the plans I had hung my future on, only to have them pulled out from under me. I took another bite, but my hunger had vanished.

I put down my half sandwich. "That makes sense when you're on vacation." She was probably only here for a few days, maybe a week.

She darted a look at me, then let it flit away, as if considering whether to trust me. Finally, she caught my eyes again. "Yes, well, I want to spend as much time that I can here. But

I might rent a car and, I don't know, take a day trip. Not sure." She glanced out to the harbor. A pelican circled the water then dove in headfirst, surfacing within seconds, a fish lunch in its bill. Did she know this was a regular occurrence? I guzzled some water and smiled at her. "I'm impressed by your enthusiasm. Admittedly I'm usually too busy to take in the sights around here, but something tells me you'll be able to give me a history of this place by the time you leave."

She leaned her head for a moment, her eyes really seeming to focus on him. "That's surprising. What do you do that's got you so preoccupied?"

I capped my water bottle. "Pathologist. I spend most days studying samples and writing reports."

"Sounds interesting."

She was trying. He'd give her that. I leaned forward, taking in her earnestness, and not wanting to disappoint her with my truths. "If I can help somebody early in their diagnosis, then all the time I spend in the lab is worth it."

"That's truly worthy work." She paused before adding, "I'm sure you help more people than you know."

"Enough about me. Tell me about—"

Her phone buzzed, interrupting my attempt to shift the direction of this conversation. Concern etched her face, and she snapped a guarded look at me. "I'm sorry but I should probably take this."

She began cleaning up when I stopped her. "I've got it. Thanks for lunch."

Greta nodded and wandered away, phone in ear. I cleared away our trash and walked it over to a public trashcan. Another pelican circled the water and made a deep dive right in front of me. Second time in one afternoon.

By the time I glanced back over my shoulder. Greta was

half-way across the street, heading quickly toward her rental. The imagery was not lost on me. Not one bit. She'd be leaving soon, and I couldn't allow my head to forget that.

A breeze picked up and I pulled that sweatshirt back down over my head, thankful for daily reminders to keep my eyes on the future—and not on the past.

---

## Greta

I'D SPENT the last few minutes reassuring Clara that I was doing well, but she kept asking me for a safe word. When I reminded her that we had never actually set one up, she relaxed. Because, of course, that was true.

"So," Clara was saying, "you're absolutely sure that Carter Blue is on the up and up? Because I still think he looks shady."

I laughed harder than the first time she'd said that. A big difference between us. I may be the more outspoken or adventurous, in her words, but she's the creative one. She has proven this by all the outlandish ideas she comes up with that never seem to slow.

"May I remind you that I looked him up?" she said. "Nobody is that pretty *and* safe!"

I was carrying towels to the tiny laundry room now, laughing my head off.

"What's so funny?"

"Nothing." I stopped, leaning on the washer. "It's just that this neighbor next door called Carter Pretty Boy yesterday."

"I'm with your neighbor," Clara said. "Trust me, you know that I always add a limp or a lazy eye to my heroes. Makes them normal. That guy, I don't know, Greta. Seems way too perfect to me."

"Hm. I hadn't really noticed anything like that."

"Liar."

I dropped the pile of towels into the washer and sighed. "Seriously, Clara, what's really going on with you? Is everything okay at home?"

My sister grew quiet, a sure sign that something bothered her. She was probably needling her bottom lip while trying to decide how to answer me. She did that often while ironing out a plot point or some other problem with her manuscript.

"Okay, fine, I give. I've been worried about Grams these days. She seems to be slipping more than usual."

"How so?" I measured out detergent, pressed a few buttons, shut the lid, and walked out.

"Well, for one thing, she keeps asking about you."

"That's sweet."

"She's been calling you Elizabeth."

I paused. "As in, her mother? How do you know she's talking about me and not, you know, just reminiscing?"

A garbled sigh flew out of my sister. Drama queen. "Because she keeps asking if you like the place you're staying in and if you've gone surfing yet, and when you'll be returning from Hollywood by the Sea. But then all of a sudden, she goes on and on about how the lure of the place just may keep you there ... the debonair men ... the money ... the fame. It's just ... weird. She obviously starts off talking about you but then goes to some other place."

My heart sank. "Have you been over to see her?"

Pause. "No."

Speaking of people who need to get out more ...

"Listen, hon, I think—" A tap on my window startled me. Carter grinned from behind the smudgy glass, holding up a couple of wineglasses and a bottle. Seriously? It was, what, two o'clock in the afternoon?

"Just spill it," Clara said, pulling me back. "You think I'm the one who's losing it, don't you, Greta. You never say it, but I can tell you're thinking it!"

I forced myself to laugh, hoping to diffuse this quickly. "I'm not thinking that at all. Can I call you back? The landlord is on the porch, and I need to see what he wants."

"Pretty boy? Did I not tell you he was sketchy? Let me stay on the line while you answer."

I sputtered. "I will not. Stop with the crazy. I'll call you later. Promise."

"But—"

"Bye!"

Carter gave me a patient smile when I opened the door. "It's five o'clock somewhere, eh?" He held up the bottle.

"Indiana, to be exact."

"Precisely." He gestured toward the bistro table and chairs near the edge of the deck. "Let's have some wine, and I'll tell you about Hollywood Beach. Unless you have somewhere else to be?"

I shrugged and stepped outside. "Now is as good a time as any."

After he poured the wine, he sat back, took a sip, and released a sigh. He crossed his leg over his knee, revealing argyle socks beneath dark jeans. His face looked young, not baby-faced exactly, but he appeared to be in his mid-thirties, at most. Yet he had an air of age about him. He used words in his emails that made me think he was from another era, or maybe that was confidence talking. He seemed to have a lot of that.

He lifted his glass. "To Prohibition."

"Excuse me? You want me to drink to *not* drinking?"

He threw his head back and laughed, then swiped his fingers across spikes of blond hair. "This area became alive during Prohibition." He pointed to the south. "Illegal hooch was found in some sand dunes down there. I believe the concoction was named "Breath of Hollywood Giggle Soup" or something preposterous like that."

Preposterous? "You can't be serious."

"Oh, but I am. So was law enforcement. Not long after, or so the tale is told, a sting op was set up to catch those wily rum runners." He sipped his wine and smiled. He seemed to assess me, and I wasn't exactly sure what to make of that. For a moment, I thought he was waiting for me to jump into the conversation.

He looked to the south just then. "Poor slouches thought they were delivering booze to a film company full of thirsty big-name actors. Brilliant plan on the part of the sheriff."

"Sounds pretty colorful."

He swung a gaze back at me. "I agree. It adds to the allure of this little niche of the world."

"I have to tell you that I'm ... smitten."

He froze. Thankfully I couldn't see his eyes behind those sunglasses.

"I'm smitten with the funkiness of this beach. I mean, you have million-dollar homes next to—"

"Multi-million-dollar homes."

I wrinkled my nose. He was probably right. It likely did not matter the shape or size of the house—it would be worth a lot of money just for being near the beach.

He continued. "But I know what you mean. This place is eclectic. Lots of holdovers from the past still in existence."

"I take it you're a fan of history."

He laughed at that. "Not really. I'd like to see more cohesiveness here, if truth be told. Regardless, I've heard the stories of the past a hundred times at a local bar."

"Oh, I see. So ... is that your usual hangout?"

He raised an eyebrow, as if I were questioning his morals. I didn't back down because, well, I wasn't. Just curious.

"I try to make myself known at most local establishments." He winked. "The real estate market is competitive here. I do whatever is necessary to stay at the top."

Now I understood. He was basically a walking advertisement. I smiled but quickly hid it when he caught me.

"What? You don't believe me?"

"No, of course, I do. The rum running story is a little funny, though, don't you think? Especially now while we're sitting here and—"

"Openly drinking libations?"

"You did not just use the word libations!" I put my wineglass down and began to laugh, rolling forward so as not to make a complete idiot of myself.

"Libations is a perfectly acceptable word."

I laughed again. The word trilled through my head and I laughed harder. I gulped air then snorted wine up my sinuses—which only made me double over more. I could not breathe and held onto the edge of the table to steady myself.

Carter looked unconcerned. "I take it you don't care for the wine."

I shook my head and crossed my palms in front of myself

back and forth like windshield wipers. "Stop making me laugh."

He looked unconcerned, although I detected a smirk emerging. I laughed until I could breathe easily again. "I have a question for you."

"Shoot."

"You were rather—how should I say this—terse in your emails when I contacted you about this place. But now you're up here laughing and drinking wine like ..."

"Like the friendly guy that I am?"

I took a sip. "Well, yes."

"I apologize if my emails were off-putting."

"They weren't."

"You're quite tough then." He scrutinized me with a long gaze. "You must be to come here on what would have been your honeymoon."

"Yes, well, I don't really want to talk about that."

"Understood. To answer your earlier question, I have had some opposition to my vacation rental up here."

I nodded. "From the man with the dog? Zac?"

Carter screwed up his mouth a moment before continuing. "To be fair, this area has more than its share of short-term rentals. Some visitors forget that they're staying in a neighborhood of people who are not on vacation."

"So the gruff response is how you weed through the partiers."

"Last thing I need is more trouble with the neighbors."

"Well, I promise not to be any trouble!"

Carter drained his glass and laughed. "Listen, I'm going to be showing some properties this weekend. Would you like to join? I will be sure to let my clients know you are not a competitor aiming to buy their dream property out from under them." He paused. "Unless, perhaps, you are."

"Really? I'd love to see inside some houses. No, no plans to move here, but thank you. Really. Just tell me what time and where to meet you."

We made plans to meet downstairs on Saturday morning. I didn't ask which properties he was showing, probably because I was still nursing my embarrassment over wine snorting. I was also kicking myself for not keeping him on the subject of the history of Hollywood Beach, though he himself admitted he wasn't all that interested in the past.

Anyway, who knew what I might discover on my little tour? Not every house around here had been torn down to make way for something new. It was very possible that I would find all kinds of older ones. I sighed. How great would that be?

After Carter left, I threw out the wine left over in my glass and filled a water bottle. Between that sandwich from earlier and the wine, I wasn't much hungry yet, so I jogged down the steps in search of the beach.

The tide was somewhere in the middle of low and high, still providing an easy path to walk along the shore, while also threatening at times to lap right onto dry sand. I rolled up my yoga pants and let my bare feet swish around in the water. It was warmer than I imagined it would be.

Clara and I had seen few photos of Great-gran, but in my head, she shined bigger than life. Both Mom and Grams had seen to that, I suppose, with their stories of her days as a starlet in movies filled with swashbucklers and other heroes dripping with charm. I'd always wondered why she left all that behind but asking was to question the existence of those of us who came after—few in number as we were.

Whenever I would question, Mom would simply say that our great-grandmother needed to come back to Indiana where Clara and I would someday be born. But our grandmother's face always registered something more mysterious, as if Great-gran's past was more complicated than that. I slowed, the swirl of the water around my ankles bringing a calm I didn't know I needed.

"We meet again."

I gasped and jerked a look up at Zac. He was holding out an orange slice to me.

"You shared your lunch with me, so it's the least I could do."

The man was everywhere in this small slice of the coast. It was somewhat unsettling. "Thanks." I plopped the orange into my mouth, thankful that my startled heartbeat had begun to slow.

Bubbles aka Sport galloped up from behind her owner, circled me, then stopped and shook off seawater from head to tail.

"Sport!" Zac commanded. "Stop!"

He bent and put his hand in front of the dog, as if to stop her without touching her. Apparently Sport thought his owner was playing. She leaned back on her haunches á la Downward Dog and sprang forth, leaping up to nibble Zac's nose. She barked once—obviously pleased with herself—then ran off, leaving splashes of water in her wake.

Zac gave me a chagrined look. "Sorry. I wish I had a towel to give you."

"It's just water." I looked toward the dog, who was springing through the tide like a gazelle. "Bubbles is cool with it too, apparently."

"Please."

I laughed at the way he rolled his eyes like a kid. "Ex-girl-friend's dog?"

"Yup." He looked down at the wet sand then raised his gaze to mine. "How'd you know?"

I shrugged. "A hunch. When Carter mentioned her real name the other day, you pretty much gave yourself away."

He scowled at the sound of Carter's name. Boy. That was some bad blood between those two. I tried to imagine the partiers that Carter must have opened his neighborhood to and what Zac's reaction had been.

I gestured toward Zac. "That's the face you made yesterday."

"I'd rather not talk about your landlord, if you don't mind. He doesn't know what he's talking about, by the way."

"I see. And what is he talking about?"

Zac lowered his brows, scrutinizing me. Almost as quickly, his scowling face evaporated. "Forgive me," he said. "You're on vacation, and I have no right to insert you into problems with the neighbors."

I hadn't expected him to show an about face like that. He'd changed course twice in the twenty-four hours since we met, softening his stance when something obviously both-ered him. Then again, I barely knew this man. One day and a few brief conversations wasn't enough to call us ... friends.

The tide decided to lurch forward then. Zac grabbed my hand, leading me toward dry sand, but I gently pulled myself loose from his touch. For a couple of seconds, we stood there, staring at each other. He spoke first.

"Change of subject. How are you enjoying the beach? Or is that a rhetorical question?"

"I love it here so far. What I've seen of it anyway."

"First time?"

"To the West Coast, yes. My family went to the beaches of Lake Michigan several times when I was a kid. We took a road trip to Florida once too. I was very young then. So—" I glanced around, taking it all in—"this is all truly stunning. I think I'll come out later for sunset too."

"You'll find a lot of company out here when you do."

"Oh?"

"If I'm home by then, I'd be working in my upstairs office. Through my window, I often see groups of people heading toward the beach, carrying their drink of choice with them. A few minutes later they fill up the street again on their way back home."

"I hope you join them sometimes."

"Me? No, I'm usually too engulfed in what I'm doing. I can't tell you how many times I've looked up only to discover that it's already dark."

"That's sad."

He laughed. "Not sad. Just life."

"Hm."

"Oh and keep an eye out for the green flash. It's a common phenomenon around here—or so I've heard."

I hesitated to show him my ignorance over this so-called green flash. If he were Tommy, he would launch into scientific jargon and make me feel stupidly uneducated.

It wasn't fair to compare a stranger to my ex, so I allowed myself to prod him along. "What exactly is the green flash?"

He leaned toward me now, and I could feel the light touch of his hand on my lower back. He pointed far off into the distance, his voice low. "People swear that if you're looking at just the right spot on the horizon, you'll see a green flash right as the sun sets."

I followed his gaze, trying to picture it. When he didn't

continue, I stole a look at him, his proximity startling. I looked back to the horizon, wondering if he had more to add.

"I'm sure there's a better explanation for it," he said, eventually, "but I've never researched the phenomena enough to give you any more than that."

I kept my gaze away from his, fearful he would see how I had been summing him up to be someone who knew it all—and would not hesitate to tell me that he did. But he had surprised me. In truth, I found his explanation refreshingly lacking.

"I'll watch for it," I finally said.

When Sport trotted over and nuzzled my leg, I picked her up and cuddled her close. She smelled like old fish and doggy breath.

"Now you're going to be muddy," Zac said.

"Oh, who cares." I let Sport burrow into my folded arms. I hadn't realized this at first, but Sport reminded me of the one dog we'd had as a child. Mom wasn't fond of her, but she eventually relented. Pixie followed Clara and me home one day, and we doted and fought over her, each of us vying for the affections of an animal who had more than enough love to go around.

"Better watch out." Zac ruffled Sport's drenched fur. "Or this girl will have you eating out of her paw." He laughed, as if that were absurd, and I knew he meant what he said as a compliment.

But I took it as a warning. I had come here for closure from my past with men. I'd dated non-stop until meeting Tommy. I also came for an understanding of a past that had left behind enough history to intrigue my interest.

I continued to cuddle the dog, keenly aware that, if I

weren't careful, I'd be sent spiraling off track and accomplish nothing. I could not let that happen.

---

Dearest Mother,

Something new and unexpected happened today. Ladies and gentlemen from nearby towns traveled to watch the filming of Mr. Valentino's movie. My new friends and I felt like movie stars with so many people pointing and gasping at us.

The director had to ask them to please stop talking during the scenes. (Does this remind you of anyone? Does it?). Oh! I felt so exhilarated by the audience! Not one moment is dull in California. Not one!

Please tell Father hello and that I am safe.

Lizzie

# CHAPTER SEVEN

**Greta**

THE NEXT MORNING I pulled on my old running shoes and crossed the divide between my rental and Zac's house and knocked on Helen and Gus's place. No answer. I'd been thinking about it all night. Perhaps in exchange for Gus's help with local history, I could offer them some of my organizational skills? My second knock was met with more silence.

A disembodied voice broke my concentration. "An Uber picked them up early this morning." Carter peered at me from his place at a dining table by the window. The screen was filthy. "I watched as they were squired away on a drug store run."

"How do you know that's where they were going?"

He smirked. "They always come back with a pharmacy bag and an extra roll of toilet paper."

"If that's not the sweetest thing I've heard." I paused, my joy dying down. "Was Helen able to walk okay?"

Carter frowned, as if confused by my questions. He shrugged. "I would venture a yes on that. She was using a walker with wheels—was quite rickety, though. I watched the driver fold it up for her."

"Hmm. I hope she'll be all right."

"You worry too much."

I tsked, but he only smiled and offered me a good-natured toast with a mug of something. I imagined whatever it was to be spiked with Irish whiskey or similar. I stepped out toward the street, then leaned a hand into my waist and stretched lightly. I'd forgotten to bring down the postcard to show to Gus anyway. This beautiful day called to me, and I wouldn't let myself waste it. With my plans dashed for the morning, I turned only to run into ... Zac.

"Good morning, Greta."

He looked a little nerdy with his tool belt and a hammer in his hand, but in a good way. There was an earnest look to his eye, like someone with a secret. I hadn't said anything yesterday, but Zac didn't strike me as the construction guy type. He held up the hammer, as if showing me a prize. "Thought I'd make them another ramp. For the backyard, this time."

I gasped a little. "You made the one in front here?" I gestured to the ramp leading into the front of the unit.

"I did."

"Wow. I wouldn't have guessed."

This seemed to surprise him. His laugh had an incredulous note to it.

I grinned. "I mean, it doesn't look homemade."

His laughter roared now. "You mean, like I made it in shop class? Thanks a lot."

"I just meant that ..." My thoughts tumbled over each

other, not making much sense. Where were Clara's writing skills when I needed them? She could give me just the right words to say. "You're a doctor, aren't you? Don't you have to protect your hands or something?"

"Uh, if I was a surgeon, yes I suppose I would."

"That makes sense." He hesitated visibly. Maybe he was done with pleasantries. I'd have to remember that.

"In the past," he said, "I did perform myriad outpatient procedures, but these days I spend most of my time analyzing tissue and offering my educated opinion to assist treating doctors in making informed decisions."

I let all that soak in.

"Right." He flipped the hammer into a pocket of his tool belt. "Guess that sounded somewhat pretentious."

"Not at all. It shows your versatility. It's nice of you to take care of your tenants so well."

He seemed to consider that. "Thank you." He cleared his throat. "Too bad Gus wasn't able to take you up on your offer to accompany him on a walk."

I shrugged. "I'll come back another time."

He nodded. "Indiana's a long way."

"I mean tomorrow."

"So you're here all week then?"

Though my internal safety meter, AKA my sister's voice, caused me to pause, I eventually blurted out, "I will be here for three months."

His eyes widened. "Three ... months? I hadn't realized you would be here for that long."

I licked my lips, which had suddenly gone dry. Something about the way Zac stood there looking all nerdy and vulnerable made me think he was safe, that he wouldn't laugh at my rather wild and last-minute idea of coming all the way here on a postcard and a prayer.

"Yes, well, I had a lot of vacation time saved up ..." I didn't mention that there was no job to go home to, as that would make me sound reckless. I shrugged. "And why not spend it here in this beautiful place?"

His eyebrows dipped as he seemed to search for some kind of response.

I took a step back. "I'll let you go now. Have a nice day, Zac."

But he didn't move. "I wish I shared your enthusiasm for this place." He glanced around before returning his gaze to her. "With all due respect, I would not have thought of this beach as a ..."

"A what?"

"A honeymoon spot."

I sucked in a breath. "Honestly, me either."

"Then, may I ask, what brought you here?" He paused, a small laugh coming from him. "Other than the sun and sand you don't have at home, I mean."

Though he had a smile on his face, that earnestness poked another tiny hole through the layers of reticence between us. Maybe it was his apology yesterday or the nerdy tool belt—or both—but for some reason, I was beginning to relax and feel safe. "I came here because I believe that my great grandmother once lived here. I, well, I know that she did."

"You're kidding."

"I'm not. The idea started with a postcard that my sister and I found. We'd heard about our great-gran's brief career in Hollywood, but the stories were spotty, inconsistent.

When we received the postcard, it was like the missing piece being put into place."

"So you think she lived all the way up here? Rather than in the real Hollywood?"

I allowed my gaze to meet his squarely. "Yes, I believe so."

He considered me for a good, long while, no hint of derision in his expression. "Well, then, this is exactly where you need to be, isn't it?"

"You really think so?"

"Listen, if I had the opportunity to walk in my great-grandmother's steps, I would do that in a heartbeat."

"You're not even laughing."

He pulled back, tucking his chin. "Why would I laugh about something as important as that?"

His question knocked me off balance. This wasn't Europe, where large swaths of ancient history could be found out in the open. This was the West Coast. Wouldn't most men think a woman nuts to hop on a plane to find a piece of history that had long been cleared away by progress? I took a chance in telling Zac this tiny fact about why I was here, but he had not reacted the way I had expected, the way I had feared. Not at all.

"I apologize. I guess you wouldn't."

"Listen, I have work to do in there"—he nodded toward Gus and Helen's front door—"but maybe I can help. If you'll let me."

I hesitated. He was a busy doctor. I was on vacation. I didn't want to put him out. Still, my time here was limited, so eventually I said, "Sure."

He turned to go, then pivoted back. "I've got a small boat over in the harbor. Why don't you let me take you on a cruise this weekend? The harbor might not have been here a hundred years ago but it will give you another perspective. Would you like to go?"

Again, my sister's admonition about needing other voices in my life nudged me. Maybe this was her answer. More than that, I wondered at this gift from my God, the one who, despite all my questions in life, had never failed me. I hadn't felt this carefree in months.

Zac waited, his expression expectant.

I smiled. "I would love that, Zac. Thank you so much for the offer."

He nodded, his grin almost shy. "Five o'clock Saturday work for you?"

I bit my lip. "I think so. I told Carter I'd meet him at noon, but I'm sure we'll be back in plenty of time."

He hesitated. "I see."

"He's showing houses and invited me to join him."

Zac's expression darkened as quickly as his brows dipped.

"You don't like looking at open houses?"

"Never."

Maybe this wasn't the best idea. I didn't care to get in between whatever battle those two continued to wage. "Zac?"

"Yes?"

"I know that you don't like him," I said, "but I also know that whatever has happened between you has nothing to do with me. And it's not something I even care to know about."

Zac watched me for a few seconds, a flash of indecision in his expression. I sensed he wanted to tell me his side of things, but then, he sucked on his bottom lip and nodded. The blue in his eyes had faded some.

"See you Saturday," he said.

I nodded and began to back away, when he stopped me.

"And Greta?"

"Hm?"

"Enjoy your run."

---

DEAREST MOTHER,

THE OTHER WOMEN ARE WARRING. Edith, one of the actresses, fainted from the heat today and all the other ladies wanted to replace her. She only had one word to say, Mother, but oh how I wanted the task.

I awaited my turn and, lo and behold, Mr. Valentino approached me. He asked if I would like to take her place, and I could not believe my ears!

Of course, I said yes. My heart was fluttering uncontrollably, but I stepped onto my mark and when it was my turn, I put my fingers to my mouth and said, "Oh" with as much expression as I could muster.

This could very well be described as the best day of my life. I dearly hope that my likeness will become part of the movie forever.

LIZZIE

---

**Zac**

. . .

I HATE TO ADMIT IT, but Lisa was right. This time, anyway. I lugged a tarp and the last of necessary tools down to the garage and set up shop with Sport nipping at my feet. If I was going to get those shelves built for the apartment, I needed to get busy. The list of upgrades was long: new bathroom vanity, lighting from this century, crown molding, paint, and somewhere for renters to place their things, i.e., these shelves.

Lisa had mocked my skills when we bought this fixer and I took on the smaller jobs rather than hire in a contractor for everything. "Why does it bother you so much?" I'd asked her once.

"Because you're a *doctor,*" she'd said, as if my profession prevented me from pursuing other projects.

In many ways, though, I saw her point. At times, work had been all consuming for me, the demand for answers never slowing. It had been important to me to surround myself with medical professionals who cared deeply about their patients. But with that had come a relentless search for truth. Staff would call me, then email, and then keep calling until they had what they wanted.

In many ways, working with my hands helped me to cope with the stress, but Lisa hadn't seen it that way. Sometimes, she would pout and curl up next to me, even as I attempted to make sense of an abnormality of some type.

"I never see you anymore, Zacky," she would say, "and now you want to spend more time away from me."

That pout of hers sliced me in two. One part made me want to chuck my work and marry her already. Actually, that's what I felt most of the time. But if I were honest, really, gut-wrenchingly honest, her antics often set my teeth on edge too. My jaw would literally ache after she would wear me down with her frowns and occasional bursts of tears.

It took some time apart for me to realize just how prevalent that second sensation was.

I exhaled, cleared my mind, and surveyed the garage, satisfied I had what I needed. Gus and Helen were away long enough for me to measure the walls. I'd ducked out of there before Helen could rope me in with a dinner invitation or Gus could engage me with facts from the good ol' days. I'd taken the dog for a walk so she could do her business, then left her in the safety of the house and its choice of dog beds.

For the next couple of hours, I settled into cutting boards, sanding them smooth, and applying a light stain followed by a coat of clear finish. My cell dinged with incoming messages, but I ignored them as I was officially on a sabbatical from work. Whatever that meant.

I stepped back, admiring my work. Not bad for someone who spent long hours stuck in front of a computer screen. With a drop of my paintbrush into a bucket of turpentine, I flexed my cramped fingers. The pain of stretching them felt oddly welcome, the kind of hurt that always did some good. I glanced at my phone and immediately regretted it.

Lisa had left a message.

The sense of a scowl crawling its way across my mug, hit me. Why was that? Hadn't I already been over this a hundred times? I didn't miss her, right? Still want to marry her? If she left a message begging me to take her back, would I do it?

A wave of realization rolled through me, landing in my gut. The answer to my questions was no, but to admit that would be to let go of the anger I'd been carrying.

Wasn't sure I was ready for that.

The jingle of keys caught my attention, and I looked out to see Gus in his wheelchair and Helen hobbling behind him, a pained expression on her face.

"What are you two up to?"

Helen waved me off. "Aw, we're a mess, Zachary. My knee gave out on me again."

I stepped outside. "Let me help you."

Helen leaned up against me and, once inside, collapsed onto her couch. Gus scooted up next to her, worry marring his face. A pang of sadness tugged at my insides. They reminded me of my own parents, both of whom were gone now. I made a mental note to call my brother, just to check in.

"I think we both need naps," Helen said, with Gus nodding in agreement. She looked up at me. "Would you mind bringing my cane, dear?"

"Sure thing." I found the cane in the corner and brought it to her. I assessed the elderly couple again, and I knew my plans to hang those shelves today would have to wait. So I left them to rest and headed back to the garage where I punched the voice mail symbol on my phone. No sense avoiding it any longer.

"Zacky, it's me." Lisa paused. "Well, I guess you're not there. Bummer. Maybe another time? Okay, bye now."

That was it. Nothing about me kidnapping Sport or wanting to retrieve some trinket she left behind. I leaned back against the wall of the garage and exhaled. Hearing her voice reminded me of all the things I wanted to forget. Frankly, so did that pretty boy next door, the one who'd found this fixer for Lisa for me to buy ... for Lisa. And when she'd changed her mind about marrying me and moving in here, he had no problem whisking her away to find her next dream house.

The catch-22 wasn't lost on me. If Greta had not rented from Carter, we would never have met. Unfortunately, now I had to hear about him, even see him sometimes.

I ran my hand through my hair, noting the need of a haircut. I released a scoff. What was I ... fifteen years old? I hadn't felt like this—like putting the neighborhood bully in a headlock—since I was a teenager. No wonder Greta gently let me know she would have none of it.

At least she hadn't changed her mind about the boat tour.

I rolled my neck to one side and sighed. My eyes alighted on the life jackets stacked up in the corner. I'd need to dust them off, as well as the boat's interior cushions. And maybe even pull together some snacks for our cruise.

It was just a harbor cruise, like I'd taken a dozen or so times before. Admittedly, the boat had bobbed out on that water, tied up to the dock and all alone for months. I'm not sure when my enthusiasm for the toy had waned ... no. That wasn't exactly true. Lisa cancelled our wedding, and I stopped taking it out. That's what happened.

When we were planning our marriage, she had gone on a buying frenzy, but *I* was the one who wanted the boat. Maybe in some odd way, by ignoring it for so long, I had been punishing myself.

But no more. I pulled myself up and began gathering what I needed to prep the boat for its first cruise of the summer. And I realized ... I hadn't felt this good about anything in a very long time.

# CHAPTER EIGHT

**GRETA**

I OVERSLEPT. Last evening was warm upstairs, so I threw open a window and allowed the sea's breeze to cool me some. Along with the breeze came the plaintive cry of the nearby foghorn, the sound of it like a weighted blanket, lulling me to sleep.

After coffee and a larger-than-usual breakfast, I lolled around some and then dressed to meet Carter downstairs.

He wore his signature shades along with a quirky smile, reminding me of one of the male models Clara usually has posted in her home office. More than once she'd had to explain to visitors that the cut-outs of handsome men on her wall were heroes in her novels—not her current boyfriend. I made a mental note to get a picture for her before I left.

Carter clicked the key fob to open his Mercedes, and I sent him a questioning look.

He lowered his shades. "You worried about being alone

with me?"

I laughed, maybe a little too loud, because he frowned. "Not worried," I told him, "but I'm wondering why we aren't walking."

He flashed me that bright-white grin again. "Can't let my clients think I don't have wheels."

"Ah."

He opened his own door and slapped the top of the car. "Hop in."

We pulled up in front of a house that looked more like a commercial building than someone's home. Tall, narrow, and flat windows that held no charm. I tried to hide my disappointment while I followed Carter to the front door where a young couple waited. After quick introductions, Carter opened the door and waited for us all to enter.

I gasped. This was a ... home? A three-story entryway dropped light straight from heaven onto us and the nearby stairway.

"The garage is beyond there," Carter said, pointing to a set of double doors, "and there's a full bed and bath down here for those guests who prefer not to climb stairs. On the other side of the shower wall is an outdoor shower as well."

The woman responded, "So my cleaning woman won't have to continually be sweeping up sand."

"Precisely," Carter said.

From what I could tell, a house by the beach had sand on its floors twenty-four-seven. I opened my mouth to correct her, but Carter shut me down quickly with a serious look.

Upstairs were more bedrooms, two with views of the ocean, but the top floor was the show stopper. A nearly seamless window stretched across the back wall of the great room, bringing about a collective sigh.

Being the showman he was, Carter opened one arm wide to bring attention to the room's grand expanse and views. "The kitchen was positioned so that the cook can chop veggies and look out at the Channel Islands at the same time."

I laughed hard at the potential danger of that but no one else did. I glanced around to find three sets of eyes suddenly trained on me. I waved them on. "Don't mind me."

Apparently, they didn't because Carter continued to garner their attention, pointing out the home's luxurious features. I took that opportunity to wander through the place, taking note of the fine cabinetry interspersed with hammered glass fronts and counters that went on for days. After a few minutes of walking through the house, with its perfectly placed furniture and decor, I wondered if anyone had ever really lived here.

A replica of a tall ship with its many masts stood proudly on a sofa table. Probably something from a stager's storage unit. I shuddered to think about how long that would last in a home filled with children. Not that I'd been close enough to many, other than caring for young ones in the church nursery.

My mind wandered to my upcoming boat cruise with Zac. What would it feel like to be alone with him on a small boat? Awkward? Entertaining? Hopefully he wouldn't grill me about Carter. First, because there was nothing much to say, and second, I meant it when I said that I preferred not to get in the middle of their war. My mom hated gossip. Had seen enough of it in her lifetime, she always said—and would threaten to take a bar of soap to our mouths if Clara and I ever got caught spreading rumors.

We never did. Get caught, that was.

For the next few minutes, I managed to view the three bedrooms downstairs, including the main one with its drool-worthy deck. I lingered there, watching boats sailing by in the distance, their white sails popping against a baby blue sky. It struck me then how very far from home I was, but more than that, how had Great-gran felt? Was she scared ever? Lonely? Or full of life and adventure?

The tapping of footsteps approaching pulled me reluctantly out of my thoughts. I descended the stairs to the bottom floor and waited for Carter to finish his tour, and hopefully, show us all another listing.

---

As it turned out, there was no need for Carter to show more homes. By the time the young couple had reached the first floor, they'd made an offer. All cash. Carter had been giddy on the way home.

"People like that," he pointed toward the black Porsche that sped away, "practically print their own money."

"Wow." I couldn't imagine how a couple that young could have enough put aside to buy a house on the sand for cash. I tried not to think of what I was going to do when this trip was over and I would return home without a job.

Carter hooted and slapped the steering wheel with one hand. "This escrow will go fast, Greta. Mark my words. They won't even need an appraisal since they won't be applying for a loan."

Seconds later we were in his driveway, and Carter exited his car, phone attached to his ear. He jogged up the steps to his front door and then turned—as if an after thought—to wave goodbye to me. I snapped a photo for Clara's character wall, and that was that.

Watching Carter in his career element gave me much to think about, especially with my lack of work looming. Clara used to take one glance at my work desk at home and tell me she'd faint from all that paper. Once, when I had asked her to fill in for a no-show receptionist at a medical convention, she said she had become dizzy from the non-stop activity. Granted, she wrote her books while sitting in an easy chair with a laptop.

But I would remind her that event planning only looked like chaos sometimes, when actually, a day of back-to-back meetings or seminars or parties were carefully scheduled, all details ironed out to perfection.

Which is why squeezing an unplanned run in between events had disrupted my usual need for order. Surprisingly, making an exception this time hadn't bothered me. I leaned into another good stretch from my deck railing, unable to stop smiling. I'd started off on the sand, jogging toward the shoreline, all the while pushing aside the voice that told me to hang it up. Tommy's voice.

He wasn't a bad guy, he just had strong opinions, and I had given in to many of them without question. Maybe it's because I knew that, to be happily married, to become that *one* that was so coveted, something had to give. But every time I jumped on a bike instead of slipping my feet into running shoes, a little piece of me suffocated.

There's something good and pure about sacrificing for one another, especially in matters of life and death, spiritually and otherwise.

I'm starting to believe, though, that God doesn't always ask for sacrifice but to follow the path laid out before us.

Olympian Eric Liddell once said that when he ran, he felt
God's pleasure. I would never be fast like Liddell—I was far
too lazy to put myself through that kind of training misery—
oh, but that run out there on the beach just now made me
sense God more than ever. It felt as if he had been running
beside me, encouraging me to keep going.

And just the thought of that made me so very happy.

I released myself from dutiful stretches and refueled
with several gulps from my water bottle. My sweaty self had
nearly dried, the stiff breeze making sure of it. A gull called
out to me from the sky. The palm branches shuffled together,
making a song of their own.

I glanced around at this beautiful place knowing I could
get used to this life. Clara wouldn't be too happy with me,
but how could I help but wonder? "Did you love it here too,
dear Lizzie?" I whispered. If only I could go back in time, for
just a day, and be a hummingbird fluttering over a movie set,
seeing my great-gran as a young woman, trying to make her
dream a reality.

I blinked away a sudden instance of tears, my heart
turning tender. Maybe endorphins, long dormant but
suddenly released by a run on the beach, had caused me to
choke up. Or was it the closeness of the past that this place
had evoked that had made emotion rise? Whatever the
reason, I found myself clinging to the changing tides of those
emotions, the ones that seemed to rise and fall like a yo-yo on
a string.

I finished stretching and stood out on that balcony
awhile longer, soaking in the heat of the sun, trying to recall
what it was like not to have so many choices—and dreams—
at my fingertips.

# CHAPTER NINE

**GRETA**

ZAC STEPPED into the boat first and then turned to reach for me. Fog had rolled in rendering the sky colorless, but I took it as a good sign that the captain didn't look nervous. I put my hand in his, and became suddenly aware of his warm touch, the firm but gentleness of his grip. He let my hand go and gestured for me to choose where to sit. The cabin was outfitted with comfortably upholstered navy cushions with white striping and a dog at the helm, her tongue hanging out in anticipation.

"I didn't think you'd mind if I brought Sport with us."

I smiled. "Not at all."

As if to drive her presence home, Sport leapt off the console and trotted over to me. She reached her paws up to my knees, and I let my fingers sink into the coat of plush fur on her back. She licked my other hand, a thank you, I think, and dropped back down to the deck. I watched her leap onto the couch opposite me, curl into a tight circle, and promptly fall asleep.

From a compartment, Zac pulled out two mugs and set them in front of me, along with a thermos. I blinked. Why hadn't I thought to bring anything other than a sweater and sunglasses?

He unscrewed the lid and poured us each a mug of hot coffee, aromatic steam rising up. "That fog layer can zap the warmth right out of the evening. This ought to help with that." He handed me a mug and took a seat. "To your maiden voyage on the SS *Minnow*."

Tentatively, I took a sip. At least he didn't call it the *Love Boat*.

Zac proceeded to give me the grand tour without even standing. "Okay, life jackets are in the hatch over there, along with bottles of water." He rummaged around in the backpack he'd brought with him and pulled out a wrapped tray. "And something about the sea makes a person hungry, so I put together some snacks."

"You didn't."

He quirked an eyebrow. "Not a fan of snacks?"

I shook my head, guilt creeping through me. "I'm sorry I didn't think of bringing anything. I'm a little embarrassed."

His smile shone with surprise. "Don't be. You're my guest. Now"—he whipped off the plastic wrap and gave me the rundown of what he'd brought—"we have a variety of cheeses—brie, provolone, and something I can't pronounce. The crackers are gluten-free because you never know these days, oh, and I went with nuts and fruit because, frankly, you didn't strike me as an olive girl."

I set down my mug and surveyed the tray. "Those aren't simply snacks, they're crudités!"

He shrugged, a smile lingering. "Whatever they're called, dig in."

I returned his smile. "This is a beautiful spread, Zac. All of it. Thank you so much."

"My pleasure." He put his mug next to mine and stood. "You get comfortable while I start her up. You're welcome to the blankets I've pulled out of the hatch, you know, in case you get cold."

Zac took his seat at the steering wheel in the rear of the cabin. Before he pulled the boat out of its slip, he switched on wireless speakers. Soon the cabin filled with music I'd never heard before. Sport's ear twitched, as if she were assessing his musical choice.

I gave Zac a questioning glance, and he shrugged. "It's a soundtrack of movie music from the '20s. Okay with you?"

"More than okay."

He nodded once and pointed us north to a wide channel lined with boats, clarinet-heavy music serenading us on the way. Zac looked comfortable at the helm, as if he'd been doing this all of his life. I guess I should have expected that. After all, he lived in a unique peninsula situated between the wide-open ocean and a generously-sized harbor. Why wouldn't he know how to handle a vessel and be comfortable on the water?

I'm not sure what I had expected, but already my assumptions were exceeded. I wasn't cold at all. Or the least bit seasick. Or ... uncomfortable with Zac. Just the opposite.

We floated beneath a bridge that soared high enough to allow large yachts to pass beneath. Older homes lined the way, flags flying and barbecues fired up, as if this was the Fourth of July and not an ordinary evening in early summer.

I was smitten.

He slowed near a corner, and my gaze caught on a house that held sentry above us. Its warm existence drew me.

"I thought you might like that one." Zac's voice broke my concentration.

"Have you ever been inside?" I asked, then laughed. "Oh that's right—you're not a fan of open houses."

"I see what you did there." His smile was good natured.

We floated in front of the magnificent house, seemingly from another era. "It looks like it should be on Cape Cod," I said. "Or at least, the way I envision those homes." A gabled roof topped a home with dark, weathered shingles, a smattering of brick, and old-time striped awnings. I knew that if it were mine, I would sit out on that porch for days, watching boats and paddlers float by.

"I can't say that I know who lives there or when it was built, but I agree with you. I would imagine a house like that could be found somewhere in Nantucket. I've never been there, but I'd like to go. Some day."

"Hm. Me too." Our eyes met and held seconds longer than was necessary. I turned back to look at the house. "It's picturesque and evokes, I don't know, a feeling of family, maybe."

Zac stared across the water. "That's a perspective I hadn't considered."

I'd grown up around women, most of them artsy and not afraid to talk about their dreams, whether they lived them or not. I hadn't exactly inherited their draw to perform or write books, but I'd mastered the dreaming part. And though I had nothing to complain about when it came to my upbringing—other than not seeing our mom live into old age—a part of me always wondered what life might have been like for Clara and me if we'd had more family around. And perhaps a porch and a white-picket fence too.

Again, a dream.

An orchestra began to play, male and female voices harmonizing, the sound unlike anything heard streaming today. Zac joined them with a flourish, crooning along with "Am I Blue?"

A laugh bubbled up out of me. "You're having too much fun over there."

"What can I say? It's catchy."

"Ha. I'm surprised you know the words. I take it you're not in your eighties."

"Ouch. You hurt me."

I laughed at him. "I doubt that. Seriously, though, I don't think I've ever heard this song before. How did you know it? Or did you practice beforehand?"

"Yes. I came out here earlier this afternoon and memorized all the words to songs of yesteryear."

"You did not."

"True. I didn't. If you must know, recalling the words to that old song surprised me too. My parents played albums like this when I was young, maybe even this one." He zeroed in on me, catching my eye. "It's interesting what the mind remembers, even after many years have passed."

A giant "R" appeared in my mind then. It's not that I'd forgotten all about the suspicions Clara and I had, it's just, well, it felt kind of silly when attempting to say them out loud. It had been nearly a hundred years, so what did it matter if somehow our great-grandmother had been in love with Rudolph Valentino? Yet wasn't that one of the reasons I'd come all the way here? To dig and discover if that were possible? And, if so, could it be?

We turned down a new channel, this one flanked by businesses and boats on one side and residences on the other. Zac slowed and eased us next to a dock. He threw out a line, jumped out and looped the rope around a metal cleat.

I gave him a questioning glance.

He landed back into the boat, making it sway, and plopped down beside me. "I'm hungry."

"Oh." I slid away from him so I was no longer hogging the crudité platter. "Sorry."

But he put his hand out to stop me. "I'm fine. Here"—he dug plates out of his backpack—"I forgot to give you these. My fault."

I shrugged. "Hadn't stopped me."

"I noticed that."

I gasped, and he laughed in return. Sport whined in her sleep and suddenly woke. She hopped down from her comfy bed and sidled up next to Zac, who dutifully handed her a treat from his pocket then sent her back to her perch.

"My ex thought I was uncouth sometimes." He wiped his hand on a napkin. "Maybe I shouldn't mention that, but she, well, she wanted me to be more formal. Sorry, that's not me."

I took the clear plastic plate from him. He had an ex. Guess that was something we had in common. I watched as he filled up his plate with cheese, slices of salami, and pretzels, making sure none touched the other.

"Man," I said, "you were hungry."

He chuckled. He swallowed a bite and chased it down with a gulp of coffee. "Tell me what's on your mind."

I frowned. "Sorry?"

"Back there. When I said something about remembering the past, you made a face."

"I did not make a face."

He took another bite, undeterred. "Maybe I misread you, but it sure seemed like you had a thought that wouldn't leave you."

This surprised me. Weren't men usually blithely unaware? Ill-equipped to read minds? Or were those sentiments birthed from growing up around in an all-female household?

Then again, this man read blood and tissue samples for a living, so I guess minds wasn't too far-fetched. I met his eyes with mine and decided to take a risk, hoping it wouldn't lead me down the gang plank.

"Remember when I mentioned the postcard?" I asked. "The one that showed up shockingly late?"

"Well, the post office has been rather slow lately ..."

I shook my head, a smile burgeoning.

"Go on."

"The card was signed 'R.' And, well, I know this is going to sound crazy—maybe I shouldn't even be mentioning it—but we wondered, if possibly, our great-grandmother might have had a romance with ..."

He stopped chewing. "With?"

I looked him straight in the face. "Rudolph Valentino."

Zac frowned for a few seconds, until the light dawned across his face. "The famous actor?"

I nodded. "It's just, well, we know she worked on the movie that was filmed here so many years ago."

"*The Sheik.*"

"Yes! And then the writer of the postcard sounded so forlorn ..." I shrugged a little shrug. "I don't know, but we wonder if, perhaps, he was the one she loved and ultimately left."

"That's—"

"Nuts, right? I figured you'd think that."

"No, Greta. I was going to say that's intriguing." He slid his plate onto the table and wiped his hands on a napkin.

"Really? You don't think it's a crazy thing to wonder about?"

"I don't. Admittedly, it's not something that I would personally investigate, but would make for some interesting conversation over the Thanksgiving turkey."

"Oh, so you don't think it's worth chasing after then."

He shook his head. "Not necessarily. Truth is, my brother, Brax, and I would probably take that kind of information and milk it for all we could."

"What does that mean?"

He chuckled. "We wouldn't need to investigate it in order to claim it as true."

"Ah. So you think this is ... ridiculous. Don't you?"

Zac's expression sobered. "Not at all. Greta, it doesn't matter what I would do. Or what my brother would do. This finding obviously means something to you. And that's enough."

The simplicity of Zac's words coupled with the soft lull of water beneath us served to soothe away lingering self-consciousness. I licked my lips and glanced away. It wasn't every day I found myself tongue tied.

"You know," Zac began, "there's a story of a woman who dressed in black and visited Valentino's grave for many years."

I rolled my gaze back to him. Was everyone around here versed in lore from the 1920s?

He smiled, as if reading my mind. "Gus told me about that once. I'm proud of myself for remembering."

"I read that, though some have claimed to be her, her identity has never been officially confirmed."

Zac's eyes widened. "Do you think ..."

"That Great-gran was the woman in black?" I shrugged. "Oh, I doubt that. She left California many years ago, got married, had a daughter ... but, well, I can't say it hasn't crossed my mind."

Sport had finished her treat and showed up next to Zac, tail wagging. When he didn't immediately feed her, she hopped up onto the cushioned couch next to me.

"Hey there, little guy." I reached for a slice of pepperoni, but Zac protested.

"You'll never get rid of her if you do that."

I smiled and slipped her the food anyway. She settled next to me, legs behind her, paws on my lap.

Zac threw his head back. "Tremendous." He gave me what I determined to be a mock scowl.

I laughed and took a sip of water. "What's the big deal?"

He eyed me. "Have you ever had a dog?"

"One. A long time ago."

He nodded, his mouth grim. "Then perhaps you don't remember the farts."

I spurt out a dribble of water, right onto Sport's head, though she didn't take her eyes off her snack. "The *what*?"

"You have forgotten. Lucky you."

I laughed at him, thoroughly enjoying myself.

Zac's sigh was exaggerated. He untied the boat, slid behind the steering wheel, and wagged his head. "We better shove off and get the air flowing in here."

I continued to laugh as Zac started us up and we headed back into the channel.

### Dearest Mother,

I am sorry that I have not written to you for some time. I do not want you to worry when I tell you this, but I was not well. I caught a summer cold and could not stop sniffling. I almost missed two days of filming, but as fortune would have it, the coastal winds blew hard those days. All the pretend palm trees had to be removed, except for the two that blew right into the ocean! Those were ruined and had to be destroyed.

I did not want you to think my lack of responding had anything to do with Henry's letter. It was kind of you to send it to me. I will ponder the words he wrote.

I am better now, much better. The sea air has helped to heal me, and the winds have slowed to a breeze.

Mr. Valentino told me he was happy to see me so well today. I hope this assures you. I am very sad to say that my friends have mostly left me. They are angry that I was chosen to say a word in the movie.

Please pray that I will find a way to make friends again.

Lizzie

# CHAPTER TEN

**ZAC**

I LEFT my shutters open last night to hear the foghorn, but instead of hitting snooze twelve times when my alarm rang out, I shoved aside the covers and got up on the first ring. Sport snuffled about my feet as I tromped over to the kitchen in search of caffeine, probably as surprised as I was.

As the coffee brewed, I leaned my butt against the countertop. Sport yawned and exhaled a high-pitched squeal. She sneezed and blinked a few times too.

I smirked at her. "It's the new me, girl. Get used to it."

With a full mug of coffee in hand, I dunked my head in the sink, patted down my hair, and splashed water on my grizzled face. No time to mess around, I got myself dressed and headed to my workshop, AKA garage. Sport followed me, but I put a stop to that when I reached the door.

"Sorry, girl, but it's not safe in there for you." After I let her outside to pee, she sulked back in, as if knowing she wouldn't be allowed to join me.

Minutes later, the smell of fresh wood shavings engulfed me. For a few seconds, I welcomed the mixed aroma of wood and caffeine. Reminded me of when Braxton and I would help Dad with his projects. A sigh escaped me. It wasn't that grief still overtook me with each memory, like it once had. I knew I would see him and Mom again someday. Though I'd not thought as deeply about my faith in a while, it was still there, like an internal guiding light. And like the existence of people in my past, I hadn't forgotten my faith either.

Fueled up for the morning, I opened the garage door to let in some light and began laying out the shelving on the ground. Doing so would help me avoid disrupting Gus and Helen as much when it was time to put them up. Sport scratched at the door, but I ignored her.

Not too much noise this morning, and for once, Carter had impressed me with his choice in renting to Greta. Of course, I knew that after speaking with her for only a few minutes. I lingered on that thought while holding a board in one hand. Had Greta been an answer to Carter's prayers? Or mine?

The answer to that had been slowly dawning on me all night. Even more so after our boat cruise last night. We had stayed out longer than I thought we would. Greta showed a curiosity that pushed me. She didn't placate me or nod an approval listlessly. She asked questions and pointed out houses and boats I didn't remember were there. In the end, I cruised down channels that I hadn't investigated in months, some not ever, and for once in a long while, I didn't think about work or linger on my wounds.

We'd stayed out late, actually beyond the usefulness of my snacks.

"Want to grab dinner?" she'd asked on our walk back.

When I dug out my wallet, she'd stopped me. "Let me get this," she said. "As a thank you for the tour tonight."

We sat out on a bench at twilight, eating fish and chips and watching pelicans dive-bomb the channel for theirs. I'd maintained my distance with her, especially knowing that Greta had recently been cut deeply by a broken promise. If anyone knew what that felt like, it was me.

Plus, there was the ongoing realization that she would be leaving soon. A few months seemed far off when she'd first mentioned it to me. But now? The past several days had slipped by like minutes, causing me to hope the inevitable would come slowly.

"Hi, neighbor."

I looked up and grinned. Greta caught me by surprise, her smile bright, upbeat. She stood there in the morning sun wearing joggers and a form-fitting tank top. What was she trying to do to me?

"Thanks again for the cruise. All that fresh air made me sleep like a baby."

Was it wrong for me to wonder what that would look like? I tamped down my curiosity and gave her a nod. "Any time."

A whine followed by loud scratching at the door interrupted us. I frowned. "Sounds like Sport knows you're here."

"You're trying to keep her safe." She said it like she knew me.

"That's pretty much it."

"May I take her on my run?"

I twisted a look at her. "You're going out two days in a row? Aren't you on vacation?"

"It's so gorgeous this morning, I figured I'd give it a try. I probably won't go very far or run too hard. I would love Sport's company. If you don't mind?"

"Me? Not at all." I walked over to the door and stepped to the side as I opened it, preparing myself mentally for Sport to jump all over me. She didn't. Instead, the animal shot out, like from a cannon, and headed straight to Greta.

The woman didn't flinch. She bent down and scooped up Sport, who was bouncing and sniffing and crying, getting all kinds of undeserved sympathy from her. Lucky dog.

Next thing I knew, Sport was leashed and the two were off on a run down the road. If I weren't mistaken, Sport threw one last glance over her shoulder at me, her grin decidedly saying, *Sucker*.

## Greta

IN THE PAST, when I'd set out running after too much down time, I would have to take off a couple of days to recuperate. But today my energy flourished, and it might just have something to do with this adorable creature who pulled me along, throwing loving gazes over her shoulder on occasion.

Or maybe she was egging me on to hurry up. I laughed out loud. That was probably it.

Sport and I fell in step with each other until her cadence matched mine. Sport was larger than Pixie ever was, and she listened better too, but the animals shared the noble quality of loyalty. We'd bonded, and regret tugged at my heart, knowing I would be leaving my running companion behind when I left for home.

Soon, Sport stopped next to a light post that had a darkened base and squatted beside it, adding her own scent to the mix. I had the sense that we'd be making more stops like these if we stayed on the road, so after she finished, I changed direction.

We ran across an empty, sand-filled lot toward the shoreline. The soft sand slowed me down, and running across it made my calves ache, but Sport didn't seem to mind. She slowed her pace to match mine, all the while keeping her nose in the air and her ears on alert.

Surfers floated on boards out on the water, the surf showing some promise. Far beyond them, a person driving a Jet Ski skimmed the water, traveling northward. A few umbrellas had already appeared, planted in the sand like glistening lollipops. If I didn't turn around soon and spot a painter sitting before an easel, taking it all in, well, I would have to say that this was one missed opportunity.

We reached the wet, packed sand, and Sport tugged me along now, her nose hovering merely an inch above the surface. Something told me she would be snacking on sand crabs for lunch.

And just like that, she spotted one, picked it up with her teeth, gave it a few chews, then spit it out. She coughed, then sneezed heartily, and I thought she learned her lesson. But, nope, she tried to munch on another one again, so I guessed not.

"Keep all this between us, will you, Sport?" I laughed. "I

don't think your dad would be too happy with me if he knew you were out here eating sushi!"

Zac's comment about the deadliness of dog farts came to mind, and I shook my head. "No," I muttered, choking back another laugh, "he most certainly will not."

This was only my second time running in a long, long while, but already I'd re-discovered how much more could be noticed on foot. Walking did that, too, but moving quickly, allowing one's mind to bounce along with the cadence of each stride put a kind of rocket on each thought. My mind spun and whirled with each step, ever aware of the ocean to my right and the eclectic mix of houses to my left.

Peeking at houses from the shoreline almost made me feel like a Peeping Tom. Those fortunate enough to set up house with a view of the sea were also allowing an unob-structed view through their backyards and into their homes. I once heard that oceanfront home dwellers often dealt with people who leaned against the windows at night, cupping their eyes to better see inside.

No, thank you.

Sport and I reached a small, sunken beach that I hadn't noticed on my previous walk. It sat cradled near the mouth of the harbor, partially hidden by a mountain range of dunes and slight turn toward the east.

A wet child squatted in the sand, busily filling a bucket from an overloaded plastic shovel. A woman—her mom, probably—lounged on a beach towel, her face shaded by a wide-brimmed hat. The woman wore a long, breezy-looking cover-up over her swimsuit, and the modesty of it caused me to wonder what a day at the beach might have looked like when my great-grandmother was young. The few photos of swimwear I'd come across from the twenties looked nothing like anything in stores today.

We crossed the small beach until we could go no farther. One more step and we'd both be tumbling down the rocks and into the waters of the harbor mouth, the waterway that split this beach from the next. Sport whined, tried to climb down the jetty, then pulled back.

"C'mon, girl. You're going to get me in trouble now."

She whined her response, but I tugged gently on her leash, coaxing her to follow me. Instead of heading back to the house by way of the beach, we followed the edge of the waterway, past boys casting fishing lines from the rocks and beachcombers hunting for treasure. The sand ended at a cul-de-sac with nearby beach homes and a couple of businesses Zac had pointed out from our boat excursion yesterday. I knew exactly where I was now.

Apparently so did Sport because her energy surged and she began to pull me toward home, occasionally sending me a "hurry up" look over her shoulder. Up ahead, a car stopped in the middle of the street, its hazards flashing. I might not have paid much attention if the car wasn't stopped right in front of an old wooden house on the ocean side. Not too many like this one left, so my curiosity piqued.

A man stood outside of the car and pointed toward the house, while a woman leaned from the passenger side to get a look through the driver's side window. I'm not sure why this made me laugh so. I wasn't close enough to hear what he was saying yet, but in my head, it was something like, "This is it, Madge, this is the one!"

I wondered why this particular house was *it*. Or why the fictional older women in my head tended to be named

Madge. I could hear Clara in my mind saying, "Leave the story writing to me."

Ha. She was right. I was the organized one, sometimes even a bit OCD. I planned events that involved putting people, meals, presentations into place. But every once in a while, my mind would spin and dance, like our grandmother and mom often did on those icy winter nights when we'd be stuck inside for many, many days. They were vaudeville throwbacks, those two, a term my sister and I would never have understood without them.

The memory brought an unexpected lump to my throat. They were silly and funny together, but even as a little girl, I suspected a certain sadness behind their smiles.

Was that why I felt the tug of grief, even now?

"I learned to swim in the pool that used to be here," the man was saying as I approached.

I slowed and shaded my eyes, following his gaze. The place looked like a dollhouse for grownups and had a small sign out front: Windy Gables.

"Clark Gable lived there once," the man told me.

His wife groaned. "Oh, Butch, she's too young to know who that was." She opened her door now and stepped out to greet me. Or maybe to greet Sport, who she bent down to pet. "She's the cutest dog!"

"And she knows it too," I said.

"Aww." The woman stood and yelled over the top of the car to her husband, "We'd better get out of the middle of the street, hon." She shook her head, saying to me, "He likes to wax poetic about the good ol' days."

"Well, they were the greatest days," the man said. "Back then, the men were men—"

"Yeah, yeah and the women were strong," his wife quipped.

I wasn't sure if I should point out to strangers how much they had butchered those quotes. When a third car had to drive around them, the woman rolled her eyes at me before waving her husband back into the car.

I was growing thirsty and suspected that Sport probably was too, so we hustled down the street to Zac's place, passing an assortment of whimsical homes mixed with the current bland lot of contemporary-styled places. When we arrived, he was still in the garage, only now several boards were missing.

"You've made progress," I said.

"Between us, I could've been done, but"—he gestured with a nod toward the apartment door.

"Helen kept talking to you?"

"Bingo."

"She's your biggest fan, you know."

"I can't imagine why."

"She must see something in you."

He chuckled. "Yeah. A misguided soul in search of a wife."

I froze. "What was that?"

Zac's skin turned pink. "That ... that was a bad attempt at a joke."

"Hm."

He looked up. "You do that a lot."

"Do what a lot?"

"Hm," he said. "That."

I laughed at him. He looked all flustered as he tried to deflect from his earlier strange statement. "I didn't realize that Helen handled your calendar."

He cracked a smile at that. "Speaking of schedules ... "

"Ooh, nice segue."

"I was thinking about what you said about the lady in black."

"The one who visited Valentino's grave all those years?"

"That's the one. If you'd like, I can drive you to Hollywood to see where he is, uh, laid to rest."

"You want to take me to a ... graveyard."

"More like a mausoleum, but yes. If it will help you in your research."

I mulled this, unsure of why I didn't immediately take him up on his offer. A quick search of his face, looking for some kind of catch, led me to nothing.

When I didn't answer right away, he said, "You're not interested."

I broke eye contact, trying to get my bearings. My mind spun a little, but why? He was inviting me to do nothing more than sightsee, really. To take a walk into the "what if" of my family's past.

Truth was, I did want to see it. Very much so. But I was also afraid of what I might find. Until now, all this seemed like a fun adventure, a game of sorts. What if I were to go to the place where the famous Valentino was laid to rest and find something?

"I-I'd like to go. Very much so."

"Tomorrow?"

"Really? Well, sure. If you don't mind—"

"I don't." His smile was good natured.

"Okay, then, it's a date!"

He smiled at me in a young Hugh Grant kind of unsure way.

I laughed nervously, realizing I should have thought of a better word to use than *date*.

A voice from behind caught me off guard. "What's all the racket out here?"

"Hi there, Helen."

She held onto her four-pronged cane, assessing me first, then Zac. Her gray hair held a purple hue and her face a knowing smile.

Zac cut into the quiet. "Miss Greta here has slowed me down some. Sorry to keep you and Gus waiting."

"Hogwash. You two were flirting!"

"Oh, Helen," I said, shifting.

Zac wagged his head. "Not when I'm on the clock."

"Is that right? You expecting payment from us or somethin'?"

"I do recall something about you making me dinner sometime."

She poufed out her lips and nodded. "I do recall that too." Then she lifted her cane and pointed at me. "You're invited too, missy."

---

Dearest Mother,

I am feeling torn over my new life here and wishing to see you and Father again. Only one friend has returned to me. Alas, she has found a new romance, and I fear she will not have time for me.

Thankfully, I have been allowed to stay behind and watch the cinematographer work, even when there is no role for me to fill. Watching Mr. Melford and Mr. Valentino has become very meaningful to me, a director and his star. Sometimes I wonder what it would be like for my life's work to be behind the camera instead of in front of it.

I prayed for you and Father this morning. I miss seeing you both.

Lizzie

# CHAPTER ELEVEN

**Greta**

Zac drove us out of Hollywood Beach and over the bridge, seemingly away from the ocean. "I thought I'd swing you by Silver Strand before we get on the freeway."

"Oh, the beach on the other side of the harbor?"

"That's the one. I didn't ask if you'd like to. Hope that's all right with you?"

"More than all right. Thank you so much."

Our drive took us past the Seabee base and a public boat launch ramp. Zac slowed when we entered a more populated area with houses on one side and a small beach on the other.

"They call that Kiddie Beach," he said.

Given the calm water coming off the harbor, I could see why.

He pointed in the distance to where an eclectic mix of houses stood. "This area is often mistaken for Silver Strand, when it's actually part of Hollywood by the Sea. I didn't think to mention it when we were out on the boat."

I wrinkled my nose. "It is?"

"I thought it was strange, too, but apparently this harbor mouth right here"—he pointed beyond Kiddie Beach—"cut right through the middle of the area known as Hollywood by the Sea in the '60s."

We pulled up to a stop sign then that presented us with multiple outlets. He chose to follow the one that trailed alongside the harbor, eventually reaching a wide-open beach.

"Wow," I said. "Look at all the surfers!"

He nodded. "I don't come here much, but when I have, I've noticed that too."

"So this is Silver Strand?"

"It is." He continued to drive along Ocean Avenue, which was dotted with beach homes in diverse styles. "Did you know this beach was named after the silver screen?"

"Okay, that makes perfect sense, but I hadn't heard that. How did you know?"

"Research." He winced a little, like a teen who had been caught.

That teased a smile right out of me. "For this little excursion?"

He slid a glance at me. "Guilty."

I was seeing something new in my neighbor, and it intrigued me. I hardly recognized him. Was this the same gloomy—and shall I add it?—peevish guy who struck up a conversation with me in front of Carter's garden? His about-face continued to baffle me.

And, admittedly, charmed me some too.

After we'd circled Silver Strand, we found the freeway and headed south toward Los Angeles.

"I found that excursion fascinating, Zac. Thank you for the extra tour."

"My pleasure."

I sighed and laid my head against the seat rest. "This whole place is magical."

Zac laughed at that.

I eyed him. "You don't think so?"

"I don't think I'd call it magical, but you're definitely helping me to see it through a different lens."

"Happy to help."

He chuckled.

"I meant what I said. What you may find boring or old news around here, has got me fascinated."

A small smile broke out on his face.

"For example, have you seen that curio shop down the street from your house? The one that's full of different types of random bric-a-brac?"

"Yes, I think so."

"It's also kind of nautical-looking, with rope around the entry."

"If you say so."

"Plus, a little eccentric too. Sport and I were in a hurry on our run yesterday and—"

"Oh, you were, huh?"

"Yes." I laughed. "I managed to spot all kinds of things as we jogged by, like various knobs, and fish sculptures, and even a porcelain pig with a hat."

"Don't forget the empty whiskey bottles sold for storage."

I tilted my head. "Why, Zachary, you have noticed."

His expression was non-committal. "Some things aren't easy to miss."

I mulled that. If that were true, why did I so often feel

like I actually was missing something. There were days when a random thought without context would surface, like a memory that I may have dreamed. I was never really sure. Tommy would call that thought one of my *idiosyncrasies*.

"What are you thinking about over there?"

"Sorry?"

"You looked ... stressed. Do you need to make a stop?"

"You mean a pit stop?"

"We can stop whenever you need to."

I smiled. "You're sweet, but I'm fine."

"Okay."

Silence filled the cab.

"Do you like being a doctor?" I'd been wondering, but it came out like a sudden thought.

"I do."

"Hm."

He glanced over at me. "How about you? Do you enjoy event planning?"

"I love it. Or, I did until I had to cancel all the vendors for my own wedding."

"Ouch."

"Yes. It was weird. When that happens, vendors usually like to dish on the couple, you know, make predictions on what went wrong, who's to blame, that kind of thing."

"Horrible."

"Yeah. On an up note, because they knew me and our company had given them so much business in the past, I received all my deposit money back."

"Hence the trip out west."

I shrunk back. "Did you say *hence*? You sound like Carter."

He groaned. "Please don't ever say that again."

I laughed easily. "You really don't like him, do you?"

"It's not a matter of not liking a person. It's a matter of not liking what they *do*."

"You mean the lousy vacation renters?"

He went silent.

"Or is it something else?" When he didn't answer, I added, "You know what? This is too personal. Sorry. And here you are driving me all the way to Hollywood."

"No. It's fine He's just one of those guys always following the latest fad, always has some great idea to make everyone around them a bunch of money." He shrugged, his palm turning up before smacking back down on the steering wheel. "I've seen him abandon people when his schemes don't work out. That's all."

I thought about Carter and his quirky ways. He had a side vacation rental business, a nice house—well, it needed some work, but great location. He also looked the part with his fancy car and obviously thought-out apparel.

"I wouldn't have thought that about him."

"In other words, you don't believe me."

I turned to look at him, taking in the chisel to his jaw, especially when bothered by something. "I have no reason not to believe you, Zac. All I meant is that I didn't realize that about Carter."

He paused before answering. "I hope you never will."

"I'll take that as a warning."

This seemed to satisfy him. He smiled gently, though he kept his eyes on the road. It was another forty-five minutes or so before we reached the gates of Hollywood Forever Cemetery. Zac parked the SUV, hopped out, and came around to open my door even before I had finished unbuckling my seat belt.

He held out his hand to me and carried a small bag under his other arm. I took his outstretched hand and stepped down into the parking lot. We walked in silence until reaching the cemetery, but when Zac walked in one direction, I stopped him.

I touched his arm. "Now it's my turn to admit that I'd been doing research."

He gave me a questioning gaze.

"It's this way," I said with a slight laugh.

He followed me in the other direction. From what I'd read, Valentino's remains were kept in a crypt, but I'd never in my life seen anything like this one. I had always dreamed of touring Europe someday and the building looming in front of us reminded me of a miniature Roman Pantheon. Rather fitting since Valentino was born in Italy.

We wandered down the long hall flanked by markers on either side announcing whose remains were contained inside. "There."

We found the marker with Valentino's name on it. "Look at the spelling," I said.

Zac read it aloud: "Rodolfo Guglielmi Valentino, 1895 to 1926. Wow. He was so young."

"So sad. He died of an infection from a ruptured ulcer." I sighed, lingering a moment. "On a positive note, he was beloved—look at all those kiss marks on the marble. To this day!"

He quirked a look at me. "Did you bring your lipstick so you could add yours."

"Gross."

He chuckled.

I sighed again. "I love that there's a cross on his placard."

"Me too." His laughter quieted. He glanced around. "I wonder who some of these other people were."

I pointed to the placard adjacent to Valentino's. "Jean Mathis was a screen writer. Originally, Valentino's remains were in her spot."

"What?"

"It was a circus after he died, with all kinds of people calling for a memorial to be built in his honor, one where he could be buried. He had little money when he died, so June said he could be buried in her spot temporarily."

"You really did do your research."

"She died of a heart attack a year later."

"Big problem."

"Yes. So they moved Rudy to her husband's spot—with his permission, of course."

"Sounds complicated."

"I read there were still plans for the big memorial. Unfortunately, not enough money was raised, so nothing ever came of it." I turned. "Isn't that sad?"

Zac's eyes narrowed. "What about June's husband?"

"I'm trying to remember," I said. "I think I read that he was from Italy—like Valentino originally was—and that he decided to go back and spend the rest of his life there."

We stayed a few more minutes, idly looking at other markers, but always ending up back in front of Valentino's. Finally, I said, "I guess the lady in black has shirked her responsibility. I had half-expected to find a rose here, although it's not really close to his birthday yet."

"I was wondering when you would bring that up."

I tilted my chin toward him. "You did?"

He held up the bag he'd been carrying under his arm. Surely, he hadn't brought snacks to a mausoleum ... I watched him fish around inside of it, then pull out one slightly smashed red rose.

"You didn't."

He turned to me, his voice suddenly becoming quite formal. I got the impression he was trying to keep a straight face. "Greta, will you accept this rose?"

I threw my head back and laughed so loud the building's curved ceiling returned an echo. I stuck the rose into a vase next to Valentino's name, blew his placard a kiss, and then we headed out.

I didn't recognize the drive home, and Zac must've noticed my confusion.

"I thought we'd take the coast route," he said, cutting into my thoughts. "It'll take you through Malibu, you know, where all the *living* stars are."

I cracked up. "You must think I'm celeb crazy."

"Not really. But, you are a Midwest girl, so I figured you'd want to see Pacific Coast Highway at least once on your visit.

He was right. Riding shotgun on the coast highway was akin to having a front row seat to every stereotype I'd ever read about. Surfers parked at the edge of the sea peeled wetsuits off their backs, runners and cyclists played chicken with drivers in convertibles, and beautiful people wandered around in little more than a swimsuit and a tan. But the views brought the biggest smile to my face. Miles and miles of blue, undulating sea had me enraptured.

After a dip in the road, we climbed a hill until the road flattened. Zac turned east, following a winding road up another hill. "Where are we?" I asked.

"Pepperdine University."

He pulled up to the curb in front of a uniquely shaped

building—it looked like an upside down letter U. "This is the university's chapel. You might have seen it from the road."

"I did! Was wondering what it was."

"Want to go in? The stained glass in there is beautiful."

Again, he was right. The floor-to-ceiling stained glass that allowed light in from the west was a showstopper. And that ceiling! Curved wood. It wasn't lost on me that the mausoleum we'd just left had an arched ceiling, too.

Our steps landed softly as we made our way down the center aisle, a noticeable hush in the chapel. "Mind if we sit?" I asked him.

"Not at all."

He followed me into a pew, and we sat together in pregnant silence, the kind that burst with thoughts and prayers and blessed solitude. I shut my eyes, breathed deeply, and replayed the day's events in my mind. As thankful as I was to see where the rich and famous were laid to rest, this stop was a better one to end the day on. Both buildings were stunning, with some similarities, yet the inside of this one was different —it was filled with life.

Zac spoke quietly. "My parents renewed their wedding vows here. My mom loved the tree of life pattern in the stained glass."

My eyes widened. "Yes, I see it. Oh, and the open Bible in the center of it all. So beautiful. Profound."

"Yes."

Something had changed in his voice. His expression was hard to decipher. "What are you thinking about, Zac?"

He blinked rapidly, as if I'd startled him. "My parents. Their faith. How much the Bible meant to my mom, especially."

By the way he spoke in past tense about his mom, I knew. "Is your father living?"

Zac turned to me and slowly shook his head no. "They're both gone"

An ache pulled at my heart. "I'm sorry."

He nodded. "Thank you."

I wanted to ask him more about his parents, but he suddenly seemed guarded. More than once today, I'd sensed a hum of awareness between us, and I'd found myself longing to know him more.

But some things were better left for when the time was right, and so we sat, side by side, in the silence of this beautiful place. The longer we sat, soaking up the peace inside the little chapel on the hill, the more those windows seemed to come to life. I hadn't been to church since my break up with Tommy. I couldn't face the questions and the looks of empathy, as well-intentioned as they may have been.

"How about you? What's making you suddenly look so glum?"

Glum. Now there's a word that sounded every bit of its description. "I was just thinking about how long it's been since I've, you know, gone to church."

"Ah. I'm there with you. Do you miss it?"

I thought about that because it was a mixed bag. Clara hated attending, not because she didn't believe in Jesus, but because her introverted self wasn't a fan of all that handshaking and chitchat, as she called it. I loved it for the very same reasons she didn't, but I had sometimes suspected my motivations weren't aligned correctly.

"I miss what it should mean to me."

He watched me, as if waiting for more.

I smiled slightly. "Jesus has never changed, you know?"

"He's the same yesterday, today and forever."

Hearing Zac utter this simple verse of Scripture brought a lightness to my heart. It was that verse that, in the end, had won over my ever-skeptic mother. "Exactly. So why can't I be?" I laughed softly. "I seem to change my mind a lot."

He shrunk back a bit, looking me over. "I find that hard to believe."

I wasn't sure if he was being serious or not, but by the look on his face, he was. Of course, he wasn't aware of all my dating history. He knew about my broken engagement but had no idea that I'd been proposed to twice before that.

Did I really care to unload all that on him here in this chapel?

I gave him a non-committal shrug, coupled with a light laugh, enough to curtail the conversation. We reverted to a relaxed silence, absorbing the peace until students began filing in. Perceptibly, we glanced at each other and got up to leave.

On the ride home, I covered my yawn with the back of my hand, just as Zac's cellphone rang. He answered it through his Bluetooth speakers. "Hello there, Helen."

"Zac, are you driving?"

"Yes, ma'am."

"That's not safe!"

He chuckled. "We're okay, Helen. I've got you on speaker and both hands on the wheel."

"Okay, then, I'll talk fast."

Zac and I exchanged a glance.

"I'm inviting you to dinner tomorrow night. Going to invite Greta, too, if I can find her. Haven't seen her around these parts all day."

I cut in. "I'm here, Helen. I'd love to come to dinner."

Because I was staring at the radio as if it were an actual phone, I'd failed to pick up on Zac's wild gesturing. I looked at him now as he smacked a palm to his head. I raised my hands in a silent, *What?*

He put a finger to his lips and then commandeered the phone call. "We'll be there, Helen. Can't wait."

"What was that look for?" I asked after he'd hung up.

"I could've saved you, if—"

"If I'd left my mouth shut?"

He grinned. "Something like that."

# CHAPTER TWELVE

**GRETA**

THE FAMILY TABLE had been everything to Clara and me when we were little. It's where our mom and grandmother continued their antics. Our mom would usually burn something, then put the back of her hand to her forehead and say something like, "I shouldn't be allowed in the kitchen!"

To which our grandmother would reply, "Unless it's to wash the dishes!"

We would all laugh at that. Other than the four of us, we rarely shared that table with anyone else. I sometimes wondered why not, but it didn't really matter—we always had enough words and love and laughter to go around.

Clara, always the writer, liked to call us our own *ensemble cast*. For some reason, I'm reminded of those adventuresome dinners right now.

Helen leaned on her cane with one hand and swung a

spoon over her head in the other. "Everything's better with cream o' mushroom soup poured over it," she was saying.

Her husband concurred. "That's what I always say."

Zac sat across from me, and if I didn't know better, he was working hard not to make eye contact. As for me, I could see the gray soup on my plate, but I was still trying to identify what kind of meat was beneath it. Asking would surely have hurt Helen's feelings.

"Gus," Zac started, "Greta was wondering about the place with the second-hand items."

I watched Zac push his food around on his plate, careful to keep the main dish from touching the vegetables, all while waiting for Gus to finish chewing.

"Yep. That's a curious shop. You know they're sellin' an old drinking fountain in there, like the kind kids use in grade school playgrounds."

"I hadn't noticed that," I said.

Helen cut in, "Maybe they'll take your old foam coozies on consignment. I bet somebody would buy 'em."

"Hold your tongue! Those are collectibles," Gus said, to which Helen laughed.

"I bet a contractor owns it," Zac said. "Someone with leftover parts in his warehouse."

"Could be." Gus took another bite and held up his empty fork for his wife to see, sending her a wink as he did.

I stirred my food with my fork. "I will say that it's a whimsical place. Whoever owns it has a lot of character and imagination."

"Speakin' of imagination," Gus said, "this entire town is built on it. It's in the genes of the place."

"Tell me more about that," I said.

"Oh boy," Helen said, in mock despair. "Now you've done it."

Gus hushed her. "Like I told you when we met, *The Sheik* was filmed just down the street from here. Made that Rudy Valentino famous."

I nodded. "Zac and I saw his grave yesterday."

Gus grimaced. "Come again?"

Zac said, "Found myself with some time on my hands yesterday, so we drove down to Hollywood to see, uh—"

"The crypt!" Helen said it like the title of a horror movie.

Any appetite I had left had disappeared. "I don't know much about the movie, really, but seeing the gravesite was fascinating," I said. "A lot of stars are buried there."

"I've heard that," Helen blurted. "Chaplin, Fairbanks, oh, and that gangster, what was his name ...?"

"Bugsy Malone," Gus said.

"Oh!" I swiveled in my chair and pulled the copy of Great-gran's postcard out of my purse. I handed it across the table to Gus. He turned it over as Helen craned to see it.

"Oh my word," she said. "This should be in a museum."

"Looks mighty official." Gus tilted a look at me. "No offense, but that Valentino had a reputation with the ladies."

"It's crazy to think about," I said.

"Yes, indeed-y. Course, the postcard could've been from someone else, like Richard—

"Or Ryan," Helen cut in.

I smiled. Gus handed the card back to me. "Feeling honored to have the descendant of a bona fide starlet in our midst."

I laughed easily at this. "So," I asked, "have you ever seen *The Sheik*? It's a hundred years old, I read."

Gus narrowed his eyes. "You and Helen ... always giving me grief about my age!"

I waved my hand back and forth. "No, not at all. I just, well, I thought maybe you were a fan of silent films or something."

"Look at her Gus," Helen said. "So diplomatic."

Zac chuckled, and I sent him a hard stare. He stuck a bite of food in his mouth in a hurry. That would teach him.

"Okay, I'll answer the question, doll face," Gus said. "But I will warn you, your ears might burn after I tell you."

Forget about my ears, my face was getting hot, mostly from the laughter I kept tamped down inside of myself.

"It was real steamy in its day. Based on a book, but the studio heads were worried. Made them change the story. Didn't want any steam in their movie, no sirree."

I had stopped, totally absorbed by this news. For some reason, I had always conjured the image of yesteryear in clean and innocent terms. Not sure why, because even the Bible has its share of stories that could make me blush. Grams would say I should skip those parts. Then she'd frown when my mom would sing out, "Why not just skip the whole thing, darlin'?"

Gus's voice brought me back to the present. "So as I was saying, it's about a sheik who tries to force his attentions on this young adventurous gal. Well, wouldn't you know, she gets captured by the bad guys and—lo and behold—guess who risks his life to save her?"

Silence.

Gus gestured to me.

I grinned. "The sheik?"

"Bingo, young lady." He nodded his approval. "Of course, she fell madly in love with him after that."

"I would've too!" Helen added.

I rubbed my lips together, laughing lightly. All the qualms I had about coming here were dashed by these two warm and funny entertainers.

I took a sip of water before saying, "I heard that some of the street names, like Los Feliz and Sunset, were named after streets in Los Angeles so that actors on long shoots wouldn't become homesick."

Gus looked thoughtful for a moment.

"That's what you call lore, young lady. I don't think it's true because those streets were laid out after *The Sheik* was filmed."

"Oh." I tried to hide my disappointment. That would mean my great-grandmother would never have seen any of them.

Zac said, "Is it possible that it's true, but only applied to actors in films made after *The Sheik*?"

"Not probable. The developers of the areas around here—you know it was mostly just two big ranches back then—well, they flattened most of the dunes. One even added a five-acre lake a few yards from the shore, if you can believe that." He sighed. "With the dunes gone, the studios weren't so interested in the area anymore. Can't pretend you're in the Arabian desert with all that water in the background!"

"I wonder where the actors did stay," I said.

"My guess is they camped on the beach," Gus said. "Wasn't against the law then."

I laughed. "Camped?" For some reason, I couldn't imagine my great-gran camping.

"Sure," Gus said. "Why not? Movies were a lot easier to make back then before they had to schlep around so much equipment. My sources say all *The Sheik* needed was sand dunes, paper mâché palm trees, and natural light."

"Ha!" Helen said. "Your sources? Who would that be—the library?"

Gus leaned over and tweaked Helen's cheek, but she slapped his hand away, in a good-natured way. "Maybe the people who didn't camp stayed in the Duck Pond."

"That's right." Gus speared another bite of mystery meat. "Rumor has it there was a sort of bath house there. I've also heard there was a motel with a few dozen rooms in it at some point but can't confirm it."

By now, Zac had managed to squash the mysterious protein so hard against the side of his dish that it appeared he had actually eaten some. I wasn't that talented and finally opted to nibble at it. I came to the conclusion that we were having chicken. Pretty sure of it.

Helen must have noticed the empty spot on Zac's plate. She lifted the lid of the dish and dunked a large spoon inside. "Zachary, hold up your plate."

This time I wouldn't allow him to look away. I widened my eyes in his direction and caught him bite his bottom lip in an all-out effort to avoid certain laughter.

He put his plate down again, a fresh pile of whatever beckoning him. Not sure what stood out as funnier, the food —I think I might have spotted a chunk of apple in there—or the forlorn way he looked at it.

"So, Zac, you're sure around a lot more than usual." Gus looked at me, though he was talking to Zac.

Helen turned to me. "We hardly saw this guy after he bought the place and we moved in here."

Gus nodded. "We saw plenty of that Lisa, though."

Helen smacked her hand on top of Gus's. "Hush. It's not

polite to bring up old girlfriends in front of, you know, the new one."

I coughed and grabbed for my water.

Zac slid a look at me, his expression equally taken aback. I'm not sure if it was from the mention of a sore subject or the assumption that he and I were a *thing*.

I spoke. "We're not, I mean, Zac and I aren't—"

"We're friends," Zac said, cutting in. "At least I hope we can say that." He speared me with a look.

"We can," I said. "He's been, uh, surprisingly helpful."

Zac gasped this time, the sound of it like mock laughter. "Surprisingly?"

Helen nodded. "Old Gus and I could say the same thing about him!"

"Who you callin' old?" Gus cut in.

When the laughter died away, Helen reached for Zac's plate. "I see a blank spot I need to fill."

Zac pushed away from the table and patted his stomach liberally. "Thank you, Helen, but I'm full. Can't eat another bite."

"Then how about some ice cream? You have room for dessert now, don'tcha?"

Zac looked to me for assistance, so I said, "Thank you, Helen, but I'm quite full too. You provided a lovely meal."

"Kids today." Helen shook her head. "Always watching their figures!"

After she wandered away, Zac mouthed *thank you*, like we were co-conspirators, and I sent him a silent *backatcha*.

---

"THAT WAS AWFUL."

"Terribly so. Hysterically awful."

Zac leaned close to me and whispered, "Hysterically?"

I nodded, my pent-up laughter ready to explode right out of me. "Ssshh. I don't want them to hear us."

Zac glanced over his shoulder quickly. Helen and Gus's door was still firmly shut. His smile was mischievous. "Wanna get a burger?"

"Now?"

"You're hungry, aren't you?"

"Starved."

Zac stepped over to his car where it sat in the driveway and released the lock. He opened the passenger door quietly. "Get in."

I ducked into the seat quickly and let the laughter that had been swelling in my lungs pour out. For the next few minutes, he drove us north along a two-lane road, the beach to our left, until we entered Ventura, the next town over from us.

"Do you like In-N-Out?"

"I've never been there, but I've always wanted to try it."

He nodded once. "You're in luck then."

We continued on through a few intersections until he slowed the car and turned right into the restaurant's driveway and stopped behind brake lights. I craned my neck to look ahead through the windshield and saw a never-ending line of those bright lights snaking through the parking lot.

"Is everyone in line for drive up?"

"Sure are."

"Wow, we chose a busy night."

"It's like this every night."

I turned to see if he was being serious. By the deliberate nod he gave me, I knew that he was. *Wow.*

"I don't mind it so much," he broached. "Do you? We'll be here a while."

I gave him a slow nod. "That's fine." I brushed aside the thought that maybe I was becoming a little too comfortable with Zac.

He cleared his throat. "So you've mentioned a couple of times that you live with your sister."

"I do."

"Have you always lived together?"

"You mean, since infancy?"

He paused, as if to judge whether or not I was being serious. We caught eyes, and he chuckled. "Actually, I meant as adults."

I settled back against the leather seats of his car, feeling myself relax. "We live in our family home. Our great-grandmother left it to her daughter, our grandmother. But when she became ill and had to enter a long-term care facility, she signed a quitclaim deed, giving the house to my mom."

He nodded. "So it's your mother's home."

I met his gaze. "It would be, if she were still living."

"Oh. I see."

"Cancer."

"I'm sorry, Greta."

A tiny sigh escaped me, but I gave him a sad little smile as well. "Me too. She was something. I'm very grateful Clara and I were able to stay in our home. It's quite close to where our grandmother lives now."

"That's good. Do you have other family nearby too?"

"Not really. Well, a few cousins on my father's side. I never really knew him, but they're nice."

Silence landed between us for a few long breaths, until I said, "I really know how to kill a party, don't I?"

He laughed outright. "Not at all. I was the one giving you the third degree after all."

"What about you?" I asked. "Where are you from?"

He moved forward a car length, his smile somewhat rueful. "I grew up in the Valley—that's an inland area south of here, but closer to LA."

"You mentioned a brother. Is he there now?"

"No."

"What's he like?"

"Brax? He's ... well, he's kind of an enigma. He's got a great heart, a good guy, but sometimes, he's ... off the wall."

"How so?"

Zac swiveled in his seat, leaning an arm on the steering wheel. He washed his gaze over me more fully now, a slight deepening to the dimple in his cheek. "My brother never met an open road he didn't like."

"So he's not around very much."

"No, not much. But when he is, it's like we're kids again, getting into trouble." He paused and dropped his gaze. "Sometimes in my head I can still hear our mom yelling at us to get out of the house."

"You might want to get that checked."

He lifted his chin in surprise, then laughed.

I pressed him. "Why did your mom want you out of the house?"

"Because she knew that if we didn't leave soon, something would break or someone would get hurt."

I laughed lightly. "Sounds to me like she'd seen that a time or two."

"I'll say."

The driver behind us gently honked his car's horn. Zac waved his acknowledgment and pulled forward.

"So this brother of yours," I said, "is he married?"

"No. My little brother is what some might call a bad boy."

"You mean, he steals cars or ...?"

He chuckled. "Not exactly. As our mom once put it, he's a love 'em and leave 'em kind of guy." He paused. "She spent many nights on her knees praying for him."

"And for you too, I'm sure."

"Maybe."

"No, not maybe—I'm sure you were included in those prayers, Zac." I paused, watching his expression change when he didn't realize I was looking. "Unless, of course, you were much too perfect already."

"Somebody had to be."

"Hm."

He gave me that small laugh again. "All I meant is that Brax needed the prayers more than I did."

I knew that wasn't even close to being true. Every child needed prayer. Even the ones who held their stiff upper lip high. I sat back again. "Sounds like your mom was a sweetheart," I said. "A mother's prayers are so potent. Who knows? Maybe your little brother just hasn't met the right woman."

"Well, according to Mom, Brax could've had any one he wanted, could set down roots and raise a family. All of that, but"—he shook his head—"I don't know. She always said that he was running from something."

"Hm."

"What hm?"

"You care. I think that's nice." Truth was, I could relate

to the running away idea. Again and again, though I appeared to be happy with Tommy, I found myself considering the same thing. And it wasn't the first time.

Zac turned his gaze to the car in front of us, which had inched up again. In the shadows, I couldn't tell if I'd embarrassed him. I very well might have because there was a gentleness to Zac in the way he spoke about his family. It struck me tonight, more than ever, how first impressions really should not be the end all.

Thinking about that first impression caused me to laugh out loud.

Zac looked me straight in the face. "Something funny?"

"As a matter of fact, yes."

"Care to share?"

"Uh"—I smiled broadly, "I was, uh, just thinking of that first day I met you."

He groaned.

I patted his shoulder. "Okay, now, wait a minute, wait a minute. I was thinking about how first impressions"— I drew the word out for emphasis—"aren't always to be believed."

Zac threw his head back, laughing. He did not at all resemble the man I'd met that first day.

I suspected he had more to say, but it was our turn to order. When he asked me what I wanted, I hesitated. My first inclination was to let him do the choosing since he seemed to know this place well. But then I flashed back on a time when Tommy insisted that I try lamb at a Greek restaurant. I never liked lamb, nor even the thought of it. In fact, I did like chicken gyros and really wanted one. For some reason, though, I also wanted Tommy to feel good about his choices, so I relented.

And I hated every bite.

Quickly, I browsed the brightly lit white-and-red menu. "I'll have a double-double with cheese and grilled onions." Both of Zac's eyebrows stretched upward. "Please."

He grinned, placed his own order, and waited for the cashier to read it all back to us. He pulled forward again, waiting until it was our turn to pay and pick up our food.

At the window, he turned and handed me the rectangular box with our burgers and fries in it and placed our drinks in the cupholders.

"I was thinking we could drive up to a nice spot near here. Okay with you?"

"Sounds perfect."

A short distance away, he tried to enter a parking lot. Closed. He twisted his mouth, but quickly swung a U-turn and parked along the curb with a sign above it announcing Surf Check.

I surveyed the sky through the windshield, mere shades lighter than the inky sea. "I can't imagine there'd be surfers out there in the dark."

He unhooked his seatbelt and opened the driver's side door. "You'll be surprised then. Want to bring the burgers? I'll get the drinks."

I followed him across a small parking lot to a path along the ocean's edge. The pathway had crumbled some, so he offered me the crook of his arm. After scrambling down the rocks, we found a couple of flat places to sit, a burger in one hand, a drink in the other.

"Look out there," he said. "You might have to squint a little."

"Surfers! That's pretty ... adventurous."

"It is. Couldn't have done it last night in all that fog." He looked up. "But that moon up there is giving them all kinds of light."

"Wow."

"Yes, it's impressive."

"No, I mean, this burger." I had taken a bite and swallowed it fully. "It's wow."

He chuckled. "You'll get no argument from me."

The crisp night air washed over us as we ate and mused, no pretense evident. Dating was hard. Admittedly, I probably dated too often. Truth was, I could never really relax into one enough for it to be completely enjoyable. Maybe that's why I dated Tommy as long as I did and allowed us to become exclusive. Because, in some ways, he made it easy. I rarely had to make a decision for myself.

This was unlike any date I'd ever been on, but maybe that's because it wasn't actually a date-date. More like a co-conspirator meeting over a well-earned meal.

I glanced at Zac, watching as he carefully dipped a fry into the squirt of ketchup next to his half-eaten burger. He tossed the fry into his mouth and swiveled a look out toward the sea. A wave was cresting, its blue-white edging lighting up the water.

He returned his attention to his food, grabbing another fry from the mound.

"Be careful there, skippy," I said. "Looks like your fries are touching your hamburger."

"What?" His voice was tinged with surprise.

"Yeah," I said solemnly. "Too bad we couldn't get one of these cardboard boxes with dividers, like those paper plates with those little compartments for the different foods."

He looked upward. "Ah. I see where this is headed."

"You don't let your foods touch."

"Well, that's because ... it's not permitted." His expression was sober.

"Hm."

"No *hm*."

I quirked a small smile, goading him on. "Who says?"

He took a bite and sent me a closed-mouth smile before swallowing. "I do."

I shook my head, still smiling, and dusted off my hands.

"Finished already?"

"It was delicious."

"I should hope so. I would have hated for you to think that you had to polish off a double cheeseburger you disliked for my sake."

"Are you saying I'm fat?"

He sputtered, which made me laugh. I also couldn't help but linger on what he said, too, that basically, he wouldn't want me to tough things out for his sake.

Zac shook his head while wiping his mouth with a napkin. He folded it and stuffed it into the box. "You never finished telling me how you came to the conclusion that first impressions are not always what they seem."

"Oh, I don't know. I think it's pretty obvious that if the man who confronted me—"

"I wouldn't call what I did confronting."

"Okay, then, *approached* me. If that man would have invited me out for a burger, I would have swiftly declined."

"I see."

"But ... you redeemed yourself." I laughed at the look on his face, like he'd been properly schooled and didn't know what to think about that.

"I've never known anyone to ..."

To what? Talk to him like that? Tell him what she really thought?

"... give me another chance."

Ouch. My heart tugged at such a thought and suddenly my laughter dissipated. What did I know about Zac really, other than that he, too, had a broken engagement in his recent past? And that his family, like most families, had its share of problems?

"Did I say something to offend you?"

I startled. "Sorry?"

"You looked suddenly very serious."

"You surprised me, that's all."

"To borrow a word, *hm*."

I smiled.

He leaned in closer, and I didn't know if it was the stillness of the night air or his proximity, but I suddenly felt infinitely warmer. One more thing I did know about Zac was that ... I trusted him. Why, I wasn't sure.

"Earlier you were telling me about your first impression of me." He paused, his gaze steady on me. "Would you like to know what I noticed about you?"

"That I was good with gardening tools?"

"No."

"Um, maybe you saw my unwashed clothes and the sharp instrument in my hand and thought I was a danger?"

"Your clothes were unwashed?"

I laughed lightly. We were inches apart now, that shock of warmth lingering still. Despite the warning bells in my head, I wanted to lean into the slow rise of this feeling, not caring at all that it might lead to a place where turning back would not be an easy option. I sucked in a breath, considering my answer, when he spoke again, his voice low, husky.

"I thought you were a vision."

"A ... vision?"

He quirked a smile. "Of loveliness. And I was not too happy about it."

"I don't understand."

"I saw you, looking quite confident and graceful, determined even, and immediately figured you belonged to *him*."

"Who?"

"Him. The owner." Pause. "Carter."

I mulled this. "But you thought I was the gardener."

"Well, yes, that too."

I sighed and gave my head a slight shake. "So you're saying that you treated me poorly because you thought I was Carter's girlfriend?"

"I wouldn't say I treated your poorly."

"I would. But, well, we've been over this, and it's not nice to keep bringing it up again."

"You didn't. I did."

I glanced at him, our eyes catching. "Yes, well."

He held my gaze. "You must know that Carter and I are not on good terms. I can't imagine we ever could be."

"All because of the vacation rental? Zac, if it helps to know, there are many, many short-term rentals in Hollywood Beach, but most of them were taken for the amount of time I wanted one. Or much too exp—"

Zac reached for my hand quickly, stopping my speech mid-sentence. "I don't want to talk about Carter. Or beach rentals. Or anything else to do with either of those things, for that matter."

Words tumbled in my mind, but I swallowed them back. A sudden flock of butterflies fluttered around my insides.

"I don't know why you suddenly became the girl next door to me, Greta, but I'm ... enchanted."

He paused, as if the rest of what he wanted to say was wrestling with his tongue. Except for that initial meeting, our conversations till now had been friendly and lighthearted, only dipping below the surface once. This was something altogether different, and I couldn't say I didn't welcome it.

I didn't want to watch him struggle any longer. It wasn't in me. "Zac," I said, "you have intrigued me as well."

"Really." His voice had become huskier. He wasn't asking a question, but a plea for confirmation.

I snapped a look at him. "Yes. But ..."

"But?"

"I'm leaving soon."

He nodded, biting on his bottom lip, never taking his eyes from mine.

The roar of waves mere yards from us was no match for the thudding going on in my chest. Zac cupped my face, burying his fingers in my hair. I sucked in a breath, and leaned into his touch, letting him cradle my head with his hands. His gaze traveled slowly from my eyes to my lips.

"Tell me how you got the scar," he whispered, while rubbing his thumb over the insignificant mark I'd had for as long as I could recall.

"I was little." I was blushing now, warming with each second, an insistent memory trying to burst forth. "I don't really remember what happened, but I think it was when we were moving into our grandmother's place."

He smiled slightly, as his gaze washed over me. He leaned in then, and gently kissed that tiny scar before finding my mouth—and all thoughts of why this might not be the best idea vanished.

DEAREST MOTHER,

ARE YOU AND FATHER WELL? Is the air humid at home, or has the rain come to cool it down some?

I cannot continue to avoid what I must say. It is time that I make my confession: I have found love here, and I truly do not know what to do. My heart is aching with the deepest fondness for a gentleman whose name I shall hold in my heart.

Oh, Mother, he is wonderful! So handsome and smart. Knows a little bit about everything!

How will I tell Henry? I am especially afraid to tell Father.

Will you do it for me?

LIZZIE

# CHAPTER THIRTEEN

**ZAC**

I HADN'T PLANNED to kiss her, which was odd since I had
made it my practice to plan so much in life. I hadn't wanted
to fall for anyone again, especially so soon after Lisa. Had I
not learned my lessons where women were concerned? That
they were impulsive and quick to change their minds? I had
learned firsthand, not once, but twice, that most women left.

Perhaps that was it. Stay safe by choosing a woman who
would soon be leaving. It wouldn't hurt so much when it
happened.

Yeah, that was a whole lot of garbage.

I raked a hand through my hair and examined the scruff
on my face in the mirror. The eyes staring back at me had
their bags packed beneath them, as if they were the ones
heading out of town soon—not Greta.

Last night had been nearly perfect. I would have to
thank Gus and Helen later today, though I'd have to keep to

myself the truth about where Greta and I had gone and why. The idea to take her to a burger joint, then perch on rocks while eating them, came as a whim. She deserved better, of course. Fine dining. Front row seats at the biggest show in Los Angeles.

And yet, everything about the night, the surf, the conversation—had been perfect. Right down to the kiss that she hadn't rebuffed. I had relived that moment more than I cared to think about. At one point in the middle of the night, I heard my own voice, whispering to God, like old times. Was it possible, that for once, she would be the one to stay?

I heard nothing in return, and I was not about to guess at the answer. I glanced down at the paper I'd left on the counter. The one imperfect event of the night: the ticket the police had left on my windshield. Guess we had gone over the twenty-four-minute limit at that parking spot by the curb.

I sighed, remembering the change in Greta from the first time we had met. On that day, I'd managed to insult her, a stranger, who had come to these shores for noble reasons. I could not forget the way she had looked at me, the certain disdain in her eyes. Last night, thankfully, that all changed.

I picked up the parking ticket, noting the dollar number I now owed the courts. Yeah, it had been worth it.

---

Dearest Mother,

I hope you and Father are well.

In answer to the question you posed in your last letter,

no, I have not written to Henry. I do intend to, but I have not determined what to say.

I like my life here in California. If I could take a photo of my new life and send it to you, I am convinced you would be quite assured that my decision to come out here to follow my fondest dream was for the best.

Of course, I miss you and Father terribly. Sometimes I wish you could meet our cast and crew. Then you would see what I see. I have met many different people, their thoughts and ideas unlike my own.

I pray you are well.


Lizzie

---

## Greta


I AWOKE with his kiss on my lips. For the next few minutes, as I made coffee and scrounged for something to eat, I could think of nothing but that ... kiss.

Butterflies returned, the ones that had shown up suddenly when Zac and I were sitting out on the beach last night. As the coffee brewed, I shut my eyes and breathed in deeply. So far, this trip had been everything but ... expected.

Mug in hand, I wandered out to the deck, happy to find a sunny spot. No fog in sight. I barely noticed the sound of steps on the stairs until I looked to find Carter approaching. He wore his mirrored shades, perfectly coiffed hair, and cat-like smile.

"Good morning," he said. "I'm glad to see you are enjoying the deck."

I held up my cup. "And the coffee pot as well."

"Never touch the stuff."

I laughed. "Really? How is that possible?"

He shrugged. "I was born a morning person, much to my mother's chagrin."

"You remind me of my sister, Clara. She's up clacking away on her computer before dawn some days." I shook my head, remembering. "I'm not sure how you all can think so early, but"—I lifted my mug again—"I salute you both."

He went quiet but didn't leave. I thought about inviting him to join me, but I had become aware of my lack of a shower and makeup.

When he continued to stand there with nothing much to add, I asked, "Is there something you wanted to talk to me about?"

He stuck a casual hand in his front pocket and leaned against the house. "I don't usually bother my guests, but, yes, I would like to ask you a favor, Greta."

I sat up a little straighter.

"Before you booked your apartment, I had scheduled a designer to come in tomorrow. Place could use a little updating, would you agree?"

I thought about the dollar store nautical pictures on the wall. "I have no complaints, but I do see what you mean."

"Diplomatic."

I smiled.

"I had forgotten about my promise to the designer to show her around the place. We could do it through Face-Time, of course, but it would be so much more beneficial for her to come through and take measurements and such."

"So you'd like me to vacate?"

"Not at all." He shifted. "But if you wouldn't mind allowing her in for a quick tour of the place, I would be most grateful."

"Sure." I thought about my pile of laundry in the basket in the bedroom. "What time should I expect her, Carter?"

He looked visibly relieved. "Wonderful. She plans to arrive at one o'clock and stay for only a few minutes. I don't need to be here."

"I'd be happy to let her in. Not a problem."

"You're a peach! Thank you much."

He turned to go when I stopped him. "What is her name?"

"Oh, yes, her name is Lisa. Thanks again." And then he was gone.

---

GUS HAD MENTIONED at dinner that I should take a closer look at a house at the end of the block that, he believed, might have been built soon after movies were made. So I put on my running shoes and headed downstairs. Bicyclists were out in force today, weaving around cars and walkers through the narrow street. I imagined this might be a little of what Valentino's Italy felt like, with its bustling streets and houses built in close proximity.

I'm not sure when I first began to notice the stirrings of something amiss, but there have been many times in my life when I had this sense that something was ... off. It usually happened after reading the news or my email or having a conversation. I would go about my day, but there'd be a pulling on my heart, something dragging it down.

This was one of those moments.

As I strolled down the street, something nagged at me. I searched my mind more than once, trying to figure out what it was, when I finally landed on it: Carter's timidity this morning. He may have been hiding his eyes behind those sunglasses, but he stood so tentatively at the top of the stairs, just to ask a simple favor. He didn't strike me as someone who would usually think twice about a request like that. I liked Carter, but if I had to describe him in one word, I'd say cocky.

Today, though, he humbly asked to let his designer—Lisa, was it?—into the apartment tomorrow. Why did that niggle at me so much? Before I could delve further into my thoughts, my cellphone rang, and I answered the call.

"Greta, it's me."

"Hi, me."

"It's Clara."

I smiled, relieved to be pulled out of my jumbled musings. "Yes, I know."

"Stop messing around. This is serious."

I slowed my pace. "What is it?"

"I visited Grams yesterday."

"Is ... is she okay?" Maybe I should have called her, but so often, our grandmother no longer recalled my name. I always wondered if she would answer the phone, even if I tried to call.

"What? Yes, yes, of course. She's fine, well, a little confused maybe."

"More so than usual?"

"She actually had a really good day and sounded perfectly normal until she blurted out that Mom was worried about you."

"Wait. Me? Was she talking about me being out here? Maybe she hallucinated that she and Mom were talking or something?"

"Well, what she actually said is that Mom and that guy shouldn't fight in front of the children."

Greta sensed a twisting in her gut.

Clara continued. "I'm sure she was talking about our father, deadbeat that he was."

"Yeah, that's probably it."

"Greta!" Clara cried out. "I can't believe you got me side-tracked! The real reason I called is because I found something really cool and interesting. Grams had her Bible next to her bed."

"Naturally." I nodded, picturing it.

"You're not going to believe it."

I stopped fully now. A bicyclist whizzed by, leaving me in his wake. "Well?"

"It was a letter from R!"

"Are you ... are you serious?"

"Yes! She had it all folded up like a bookmark. It had that same handwriting on it that the postcard did, but then oddly, someone had written a Bible verse on the other side. Maybe Grams, but I'm not sure."

"Tell me you have it with you. You do, I hope."

"I'm not an idiot, Greta. I waited until she drifted off to sleep, then I borrowed the letter and made a copy in the care center's office. I kept the copy and left her the original because I didn't want to do anything that would upset her. She's so up and down these days, you know."

Clara's kindness struck me. She was often so scattered, but at times like these, she could be organized, thoughtful. "I'm so glad you thought of all that. Will you read it to me?"

"Mm-hm. Ready?"

I wandered down a beach access lane between two homes and sat on the sand. "Yes, ready."

DEAREST ELIZABETH,

I NEED you to return to me. Oh, please say you will? I can hear your lilting voice in my mind. So reasonable you are. You would make me sensible with your words.

The days here are warm and inviting, the water cool. Perhaps these things will woo you? There are times I fear that I have made the weather my idol, for I shall never leave it.

Ah, but you have made your choice. You will stand firm in how you have decided. This I know to be true. How I wish I could create some magic that would cause you to reverse your decision.

My heart is breaking. By the time you read this, it will be severed in two. How will I ever survive?

YOURS,
R

CLARA SAID, "Isn't that something? Poor R. Sounds so desperate."

"Or manipulative."

"What makes you say that?"

I wasn't sure.

"Greta? Are you there?"

"Yes, I'm still here. I just meant that maybe, just maybe, it's possible that R was actually manipulating our great-gran." I took a few breaths, sensing the onset of a dark cloud rolling through me. Made no sense, considering the weather I was currently experiencing.

"Well, that's a weird thought. I, for one, think it's romantic. I may even borrow a few lines for a future book. Why are you suddenly so negative?"

"Am I?"

"Are things not going well for you out there? Greta, maybe you've had enough of hanging out with beach rats and idle time. You know, you can come home early."

I laughed. Beach rats? Idle time? "Oh, Clara, I'm sorry if I came off sounding all Debbie Downer. I didn't mean it that way. As for R and his apparent, uh, fascination with our great-gran—"

"Ew."

I laughed lightly. "We'll never know why he sounded the way he did, of course, or even the true identity of the writer. Let me just say this: If *the* Rudolph Valentino was sending Great-gran those letters, then I'm suspicious. According to everything I've read, he could have had almost any woman he wanted. Did you know that the funeral was so full that women were climbing into the church through the windows?"

"Oh, that is so romantic! I need to write that down—"

"All I'm saying is ... maybe Great-gran recognized a con artist when she saw one, so she came home and never looked back."

"You sound like you're trying to convince yourself of that."

"Do I?"

"Yes. Because you're not usually so suspicious—that's my special talent."

I laughed at this because it was one-hundred-percent true.

"Maybe the real truth is that Great-gran left behind the love of her life to come back here and have babies with someone who was safe and kind. It's not as romantic, but it very well may be the case. And there's nothing wrong with that."

"And considering Rudolph Valentino died young, it sounds like she made the right choice."

"Oh—I almost forgot. There's a verse written on the back of the letter. Hard to make out where it's from—I haven't looked it up—but it looks like Jeremiah 31:19, maybe. It says: 'After we wandered away from you, we turned away from our sins. After we learned our lesson, we beat our chests in sorrow. We were full of shame. What we did when we were young brought dishonor on us.'"

"Wow," I whispered. "Harsh."

Clara's voice was gentle. "It's written in past tense, Greta. Maybe whoever wrote it was sorry for whatever they had done and grateful to God for his protection—despite it all."

A painful twist in my chest stemmed the tears that were attempting to force their way out. Why here? Why now? The sun was out, the ocean glimmering, yet I battled with some inner force that seemed to want to lay my sins bare before me—when all I wanted to do was forget.

Dearest Mother,

I had the most fun on set today. I was asked to stand in for the leading actress named Agnes Ayres! She and I are of similar height, and my hair is the same color as hers. I sat in her hairdresser's chair for more than an hour so that I could be made to look like her. I felt like a queen!

Mr. Winston made me laugh when he pretended to call me by her name. Even Mr. Valentino found that funny.

My feet are aching from all the time I had to stand in one place, but I am satisfied that, someday, I will be the lead actress.

Would that not be glorious?

No, I have not yet written to Henry.

Lizzie

# CHAPTER FOURTEEN

**GRETA**

THE SAND DUNES sprawled before me like endless, colorless mountains. I attempted to climb the closest one, but couldn't get a foothold. When I tried again, my feet sank deeper into oblivion. The sun shone bright overhead, causing sweat to slither its way along my temple, down my cheek, and run off my chin. I leaped into a crevice and ran to another dune, a shorter one. It looked easier than the last, but climbing it proved impossible, my steps again taking me nowhere.

Was there another way? A palm tree drooped in the distance and I made my way toward it, but the more I walked, the farther away it stood. Clouds covered the sun now, making it more difficult to see my way out of this vast maze of sand. I looked left and then right. What was supposed to be a fun adventure now peppered me with fear.

Someone called my name. Mom? Grams? The voice started off strong and loud, but as it moved closer to my hearing, it dissipated in the wind. The sound of it was familiar, achingly so, yet I could not fully grasp who was crying out. I strained to hear the words, but again, they fell away from me.

My heart quickened and I began to run now, but my feet moved as if wading through mud. The dry ground had become wet in places, but the soft sand did not spring back. Instead, with each step, I found myself sinking deeper and deeper still.

I jolted awake.

Confusion gripped me. I blinked, taking in the framed seashell art on the bedroom wall, and I exhaled, realizing.

I was on vacation, at the beach, and I had been dreaming.

I lay there in the dark, the foghorn's cry from the harbor mouth attempting to calm me. It helped some, but my heart continued to beat crazily. I knew it would take some time to come down from the vividness of my dream. Even now, I wondered, just a little bit, if any part of it had been real.

## Zac

I'D BEEN at it all morning. I had not meant to become so lost in the project plans for remodeling my tenants' place, but I'd had a surge of energy that had carried me through the hours. I glanced at my phone, surprised. Lunch time. I shut down the computer where I had been reviewing my architect's drawings and the other open tabs containing myriad choices for countertops, flooring, window coverings, et cetera, et cetera.

A hitch in my chest told me the truth: It wasn't hunger

that had pulled my mind from the work in front of me—I was missing *her*.

I thought about foregoing food, dashing downstairs, only to climb the stairs to her place. Maybe Greta wanted to grab some lunch. We could walk over to the harbor, like that time we'd bumped into each other innocently enough.

A groan filled the air around me, and I froze. *Get a grip, Zac.* Despite the change in our relationship yesterday—it was a relationship, correct?—nothing had changed regarding Greta's plans. Nor had she accomplished her goals for coming here in the first place. What would happen once she did come to some final conclusion regarding her great-grandmother's former life in this insignificant speck on the map?

The more I thought about her answer, the more it sank like a stone in my gut. She'd leave. Go home revitalized. Probably start a new business in the hometown that knew her. It was the right and best thing for her. For me? I wasn't so sure.

A car door slammed outside. Carter's Mercedes. A definite drawback from homes built inches apart was that even the sound of car door shutting becomes familiar, something a person could actually picture in their mind.

Was it terribly odd to hate the sound of a Mercedes?

I looked out the window to see the guy twirl his keys in his hands, jam them into a pocket, and trot up to his front door stoop. Half expected to hear him humming "Zip-a-Dee-Doo-Dah" too.

"Sell another money pit to some unsuspecting sucker?" I muttered. My neighbor couldn't hear me, but saying it out loud made me feel good anyway.

I stepped away from the window, annoyed. My disdain for Carter had intensified in the past couple of weeks, and I could only think that it had to do with the fact that I was, technically, on vacation. When I spent hour after hour holed up in my home office, examining compromised tissue and writing reports, I hadn't the time, nor the inclination, to give two thoughts about the guy.

*Love one another, as I have loved you ...*

My mother's voice filled my head, though admittedly I tried to dodge it. Instead, it landed like a well-aimed punch. I groaned again, giving into the admonition to love one another. This wasn't a time for discerning God's will—I knew what it was because, well, He'd left it in written form.

Didn't mean I had to like the guy. Right?

I pushed unneighborly thoughts away, put on my shoes, and headed outdoors for fresh air and vitamin D that didn't come in pill form.

The air outside of Gus and Helen's front door hinted at burned bacon, and I forced myself not to laugh out loud. I thought about last night, realizing I should be grateful for her lack of culinary skills. Then again, how much longer would she and Gus survive on her attempts?

The door squeaked open— I made a mental note to grab some oil from the garage—and Helen poked her head out. "Good morning, Zachary."

I grinned at her use of my full name, usually reserved for my mom when she was living. "Hello, Helen."

She pursed her lips and lifted her chin, examining me through her glasses. "Was a guy skulking around here early this morning." She gestured toward the wall with a nod of her head. "Said he was an electrician. Was going to put some fancy doorbell right there."

Whoops.

"That's on me. I meant to tell you last night, but it slipped my mind."

"Zachary!" Helen stepped outside onto the ramp now and leaned on her cane. "I chased that poor fellow out of here like he was a common thief."

I chuckled. "He's a big boy. I'm sure he wasn't terribly wounded."

"Don't be so sure!" She picked up her cane and pointed it at me. "I can be rather intimidating."

I did not doubt that. I nodded, acknowledging that, yes, she could hold her own. "Rest assured that he survived. In fact, he texted me to say that he obtained the measurement he needed. He's going to install a video bell there."

"Video! Oh my word. That sounds far too technical for me and old Gus to handle."

"I'll teach you, but don't worry. It's for your protection."

A glimmer of a laugh appeared on her face. "From who? That rascal Carter?"

I was thankful for her quick wit, and for much more than that. If I were Helen, I'm not sure I could so easily forgive.

"I heard my name."

I turned around. Carter stood on the dividing line between our two properties, and while I usually wasn't one to notice what another person wore, the guy made it easy. He looked like a beachcomber from the silent movie days in his striped shirt and track pants that could use another half foot of fabric. I wanted to suggest he add a sailor hat to his ensemble but bit my tongue.

Helen picked up her cane again and pointed it in Carter's direction. "Don't eavesdrop!"

Carter crossed his arms, but his smile held a question. I wasn't sure I cared to give him the time to ask it.

"Is the good doctor giving you trouble this morning, dear Helen?"

"Zachary is taking good care of us over here, thank-you-very-much."

"Glad to hear that." Carter grinned and tipped that imaginary sailor's hat at Helen.

I stood between them, feeling tension securing itself to my neck muscles. I had intended to jog up the stairs to Greta's rental, but I wasn't counting on an audience. After a few seconds, it became clear that this was a face off—and neither of us felt any inclination to leave first.

Helen moaned. "My bones are aching. Bye, boys." She was gone, the screen door slamming shut behind her.

I swung a look back at Pretty Boy. "You can go now."

"I think I'll stay right here and enjoy the warmth of that sunshine up there," he said.

Inwardly, I fumed. Hated when that guy toyed with me. I'd been in the middle of his mess not once but twice.

Again, my mother's voice asserted itself. Inwardly, I let off some steam. Carter wasn't my favorite person, and he never would be. But he had found himself in trouble and was still digging his way out, and that had to be good enough for me.

---

**Greta**

I WANDERED down the beach until I landed squarely in front of the house Gus had mentioned at dinner the other night. There was no denying it had been there a long, long time, but it only showed its age in its design, not in its upkeep. It was ... charming. Small doorway, arched roof, Spanish tile inlaid into its stucco-exterior. The house did not have that quintessential beach house vibe. Instead, its roots were embedded in a yesteryear that I was only beginning to explore.

I stood off to the side, careful not to appear like a stalker to whomever might be peeking at me from one of the clear glass windows. We didn't have anything like this at home, and I found myself longing to know how long it had been here. Was it possible that my great grandmother had stood on this spot? Had she admired it, as I did?

Silly as the thought might be, it warmed me through and lightened my mood. I decided to continue to walk along the road until I hit the north jetty. I stopped there and sat on the rocks awhile, watching a plethora of boats, some going out to sea, others coming in. A fishing boat laden with rust, an abundant catch, and a tired-looking crew rode in on the wake of a larger vessel.

I might have stayed there all day if my bladder could have handled that. But I'd promised Carter to return by early afternoon anyway, to let his designer in. I felt rather selfish admitting this, but I had to give myself a pep talk to leave. I hadn't realized the luxury, until now, of having zero appointments to meet and a part of me was feeling stingy with my time.

It was more than that, though. I walked home on the harbor side of the peninsula, forcing myself to examine all that had been niggling earlier today. Maybe it wasn't Carter's request that had bothered me so much as my thoughts from the night before. Simply put, I had enjoyed spending time with Zac. He wasn't the curmudgeon I had originally thought. I found him strong and thoughtful, but more than that, there was a vulnerable quality to him. I saw that when he told me about his broken engagement.

I slowed my pace, heat rising in my cheeks, and not the good kind that came along with affection. It was the kind that rose with ... shame. Zac had laid his heart bare for me, told of his ruined engagement and some of the aftermath.

Part of me felt as if he'd been holding something back, but how could I judge him for that when I had kept my own heartache closely protected?

I might have explored this further if a sharp retort hadn't split the quiet of my thoughts. It was a man's voice—Zac's.

"It's time for you to pack up your mess and go."

"You would love that," Carter was saying. "Would help you with your Big Shot status."

I hadn't expected to see Carter standing outside when I returned. Isn't that the reason he wanted me to let his designer in? Because he had somewhere else to be?

I could tell by the expression on Zac's face that he was about to deliver a missive back to Carter, but he shut his mouth when our eyes caught.

"Hey there," he said.

I stepped up close to him, searching his eyes for a sign of the affection that had been there the night before. Not that I expected him to suddenly take me in his arms and kiss me right there in front of Carter. But if I were to be honest, I hoped to see desire in his face to do just that.

He unfolded the arms locked at his chest and reached out to me, giving my hand a squeeze. My heart fluttered at his touch. His eyes told me everything I wanted to know and more, which brought me both happiness and a bit of trepidation.

"Well," Carter said, interrupting the moment, "I have an appointment to make."

As he unlocked his car and opened the driver's side door, I almost wanted to ask if he'd looked in a mirror. No judgment, but he was dressed for ... what I wasn't quite sure.

Carter stopped in the street and called to me. "And, Greta? Thank you for your kind help today. Appreciate it, beautiful."

"Doing favors for the landlord?" Zac said as Carter drove away.

I laughed it off. "Something like that. What are you up to today?"

"Well"—he pulled a folded page from his back pocket and held it in the air—"I was about to take a break and grab some lunch, and then, I don't know, maybe take a ride down to the county courthouse and pay this parking ticket I received."

"Oh, ugh!" I pulled away from him. "I'm still so sorry about that."

He chuckled and pulled me closer again. "I'm not."

If there was any illusion that what I was beginning to feel for Zac last night came out only due to that gorgeous moon against a plush sapphire sky, it was shattered by this moment. It was barely noon, the sun was overhead, and in the very bright light of this day, I found myself falling even more.

He brushed my lips with his, and I tried not to think about what a problem this might become in a few short weeks.

Zac drew back slightly, though his hold on me did not lessen. His voice against my ear turned husky. "So ... about lunch."

I smiled. "Let me fix it for you."

His eyes widened, like he was about to protest, but I shushed him. "Let me. I bought groceries that, thanks to you and my sweet neighbors here, I haven't eaten much of."

He nodded. "Well, then, I accept."

———

THE SMALL COUNTER looked as if a grocery bag had exploded over it. I added a knife and cutting board to the mix of sliced ham and turkey, provolone, lettuce, tomatoes, pickles, mayo and mustard.

"You look hungry," I said to Zac, who surveyed the goods as if he had won the lottery. "The works?"

"Yes, ma'am."

"One sandwich with the works coming up. Feel free to grab a drink from the fridge, okay?"

He pulled open the fridge and grabbed a bottle of Pellegrino, holding it up to me. "Two glasses?"

I smiled. "Perfect."

He poured us each a glass of sparkling water and took a seat on one of the barstools. I made quick work of the sandwiches, cut them each in half, and served them on the whimsical plates from the cabinet.

Zac screwed up his face. "Mermaids. Figures."

This made me laugh, probably harder than it should have. I grabbed one of the glasses of sparkling water and held it up for a toast.

"To adventures," I said.

"New ones," he added.

We relaxed at the counter in the small kitchen, not bothering to wander outside to the deck. There was something unpretentious and achingly familiar about having a relaxed lunch. I didn't want the seemingly mundane moment to end.

"You put my lazy sandwiches to shame," he said, before polishing off the last bite.

"I doubt that. From what I've seen, you're Mr. Organized. I wouldn't be surprised to find a tray of pre-washed sandwich fixings waiting for you inside of your fridge, like a sub shop."

He froze. "You think I'm nerdy? That I'm OCD?"

"Don't take offense, I think I'm both of those things too." I laughed. "But, well, you also don't let your food touch, so there's that."

He wadded up his napkin into a ball and threw it onto the counter with all the force of a ... cotton ball. "I'm insulted."

"You are not."

"True." He eyed me, his expression open, engaged ... unrestrained. I kept my hands busy with clean up. Safer that way. "Greta, you've got me—"

"Knock, knock!"

We both turned toward the front door. A lithe woman in a fitted blue suit peered inside.

"My appointment!" I shoved aside the food that I was wrapping up and hurried over to the door to let her in. "Come on in," I said. "Lisa, right?"

"Yes, hello, Greta."

She strolled inside poised, professionally dressed, terribly blonde and tan—exactly what I had expected to see more of in California, but until now, hadn't encountered. Well, except maybe in Malibu. At this moment, I wished I had remembered our appointment so that I could have had enough time to shoo Zac back to his place before she got here.

"Lisa? What are you doing here?" Zac was standing now, the soft expression from seconds ago replaced with a hard glare.

To her credit, my guest looked unbothered by the peevish timbre to Zac's voice. "Hello, Zac." She looked at me, then back at him. "Carter had not mentioned I would find you here."

Maybe it was my place in the birth order chain, but I had always prided myself on being perceptive. As the oldest child in a single mom home, I tried to stay one step ahead, to always be in protective mode for my little sister—and for myself. I didn't like surprises.

I looked from one to the other, and for reasons that escaped me now, I hadn't seen this coming. Last night, Zac had mentioned the woman who had broken his heart by name. And Carter caught me off guard when he asked me to meet with his "designer."

Suddenly, I realized—they were one and the same.

Zac's arms were folded at his chest, but instead of anger, in his eyes I saw a glint of pain. "What's Pretty Boy up to now, Lisa?"

She smiled at him in a way that caused a raw chill to run up my back. Immediately, tension shot through the room.

"As you must know, Doctor, that is solely between me and my client."

"I see."

"Do you?"

I stepped between them. "I'm responsible for this rental at the moment, and I'd prefer not to get any blood on the carpet."

Zac slid a look at me, his eyes conflicted. It hurt my heart to see them. He dropped his arms to his sides and moved toward the door. "I was leaving anyway."

*No, you weren't.* I kept the thought to myself.

Lisa gave him a catlike smile—a bobcat. "Don't leave on my account, darling."

Zac ignored her, looking to me. "Let's talk later, Greta."

I breezed past Lisa and put my hand on the door. I wanted to give Zac some assurance he surely needed, plus, admittedly, hoped to keep him from slamming it behind him. His back was to me when I whispered, "I had no idea."

He turned slowly, his voice controlled, his eyes suddenly very, very dark. "I hate that guy."

I swallowed, unprepared for his venom.

"See you later," he said. And he disappeared downstairs.

I returned to the living room feeling very much like the gardener who had walked in on a marital spat.

"He always was a hot head," Lisa said. "It's unfortunate."

I raised my palms in surrender. "I really don't need to know."

One of Lisa's painted brows lifted. "Oh really?" She glanced at the mess of food on the counter. "Looks to me as if you do. Need to know, I mean."

Subconsciously, I stepped over to the kitchen and began cleaning up. "Carter mentioned that you were here to take some measurements? Feel free to move about. I'll stay out of your way." *And maybe you can leave in a hurry.*

"Zac is a workaholic, you know. Selfish. Has his own pursuits in mind at all times."

I stopped and forced a look at her. "Why are you telling me this?"

She offered up a small shrug. "Because you look as if you need the truth."

"The truth."

Her expression turned grim, pained almost, and then she blew out a sigh. "I wish someone had been honest with me about him at the start," she said. "I might have saved myself from a lot of heartbreak."

My heart thudded low, the kind of sensation one feels when deep disappointment rears its head. She looked ... sincere.

Lisa must have noticed my reaction because she suddenly brightened and looked around. "Well, enough about the bad news, Greta. This place is, how should I put it? In need of a spruce?"

"I call it Garage Sale Bachelor Pad."

"That's it!" She laughed heartily now. "I have my work cut out for me, now, don't I?"

"Oh, it's not that bad. Really."

"You sound charitable. No matter. I'll make it fabulous. Too bad you won't be around to see it."

"Hm."

She pivoted, her expression holding a question. "When will you be leaving, exactly?"

I didn't answer right away, though not doing so violated the manners my mom had instilled in me. Still, was it her business? I filled the fridge with the leftovers and turned to find Lisa waiting for my answer.

"I'll be here awhile longer," I said, waving her on, "but go ahead and do what you have to do. I will make myself scarce."

Her smile lost some of its luster. "Absolutely." She pulled out a tape measure and began to measure the space behind the couch, from the fireplace wall to the room's entry. "If you weren't just here on vacation," she said as she measured, "you and I could have been neighbors."

"Oh? Are you moving into the neighborhood?"

Lisa laughed a little, as if she were surprised by the question. "Zac knows I always wanted to live in this part of town. He wouldn't have purchased the house next door if that weren't true. You know we were engaged once."

"I had heard something like that."

"Yes, well, Zac has always hated it here. Can you imagine that? Hating the beach?"

Once, Zac told me he didn't understand the beach hype. But after getting to know him, I recognized that as his wounded heart talking. For goodness sake, the man drove me clear through Malibu. He wouldn't have voluntarily done that if he hated the ocean. Right?

It felt wrong to talk about Zac behind his back, but my protective instinct had risen up, like a shield. She had already made veiled disparaging remarks about his workaholic ways, though to me, they sounded rather benign. Could I allow more?

"Listen, Lisa, I'm not interested in discussing Zac, but I'm happy to talk about your plans to move back. In the short time that I've vacationed here, I can see why you would want to do that. It's lovely."

She straightened. "Ah, a woman after my own heart!"

"Yes, well, Hollywood Beach is a treasure." I wasn't about to tell her about my roots here, as I feared she would laugh those away somehow.

"So you understand why I intend to buy Zac out then?"

I stopped suddenly, like a needle scratching an album. "Buy him out? No, I hadn't heard that."

"It's the least I could do after convincing the poor guy to buy that beat-up house. I would have done so earlier, but it wasn't until recently that I acquired the funds to make the purchase." She said the words with the conviction of someone who believed them. "Thanks to Carter."

"Carter? Is he your business partner?

Lisa wrinkled her brows, and I suddenly felt as if I were asking a dumb question. I took this as my time to leave her alone for the duration.

But as I crossed the room, she said, "Is that your way of asking if he and I are lovers?"

"What? No!" I laughed off her suggestion. "You said he helped you obtain the funds you needed, so I, well, I thought ..."

"That was a joke. No, Carter found me a fixer upper to flip in a less expensive neighborhood. A real steal. The people had been clients of his and they were simply desperate to sell. So I hired a handyman to put a few coats of paint on it, fix a light or two, and then I turned it around quickly. I don't know why more people don't do it."

"Right. He's a Realtor."

"We met when he found me—us—the house next door. Seriously, you should have seen that disaster of a place!"

Zac had hinted that he'd fixed it up some, in his scant off hours, but a fixer? Maybe he hadn't told me the extent of its needs.

Lisa continued. "I warned Zac that, with his schedule, remodeling would be tough, but he wanted to take it all on. Well, a lot of it, anyway." She shook her head. "I should have put one of my boots down and said no, but"—she shrugged —"what can I say? He was determined to see it through."

"Admirable quality."

"Except that it ultimately broke us up."

I'd been standing by the front door, stuck in that place between politely leaving the woman to do her work and fearing that my leaving in the middle of a conversation would be taken for rudeness.

But this conversation had turned far too personal where Zac was concerned. He alone should be the one to tell me what transpired between Lisa and him—if that was what he chose to do.

I pushed the screen door opened toward the front deck. "I won't keep you, Lisa. I'll wait outside until you're finished taking the measurements you need."

"All-righty!" Her voice had turned overly cheery. "Do say hello to Gus and Helen next door, if you see them while you're out there."

I frowned, one foot out the door. "I will." I should have stopped there. Unfortunately, I added, "I'd forgotten that you probably knew those sweet renters."

She laughed forcefully. "Don't you know? They were the owners of the house. Zac bought it from them, well, after Carter told me about their bad luck."

Gus and Helen had once owned the house next door? My face must have clearly displayed my shock at that news.

"Oh my yes," Lisa continued, measuring as she did, "you really are in the dark. The truth is, they had made some very bad investments and, well, those things caught up with them."

My heart ached for Gus and Helen. How sad to lose their home that way.

"Of course, it was my idea that they be allowed to rent the lockout in front." She peeled a look at me. "Took a little convincing on my part, but Zac finally came around."

"What do you mean? He wasn't interested in having renters?"

"Not if it meant they could hardly pay the rent."

I stared at her, remembering the day Zac showed up around the end of the month and Helen had promised she'd be paying him soon. I had put that moment out of my head until now.

Lisa had moved to the sparsely furnished dining area to measure, and she kept talking. "Carter tells me Zac's been doing some work in there. My guess is he's going to give them the bounce. Ooh, boy, he could get a lot more rent for that apartment, even though it's as dark as a cave in there."

My mouth had gone dry, and I was quite sure I had heard enough. My protective instincts for Gus and Helen spiked. Without another word to Lisa—no sense giving the woman more chances to open her mouth again—I stepped out onto the deck, making a beeline for the railing. From the peekaboo view, I could see the crest of a wave. It landed with an angry crash and for the first time since I had arrived in fabled Hollywood by the Sea, I longed for home.

# CHAPTER FIFTEEN

**ZAC**

PAYING the stupid parking ticket took longer than I had expected. The line had snaked outside of the office doorway and into the hall. I could have paid it online, but I don't know, I suddenly had a strong desire to get out of the neighborhood. Big surprise.

After I finished the task of throwing away money for no good reason, I shoved the car into gear more roughly than the handbook surely recommended. I didn't care. Helped me expel some of the anger simmering inside of me.

I waited at a red light, cognizant of the tension riding its way up my neck. How could this morning have gone so wrong? I released a huff of a breath, forcing my blood pressure into submission.

Seeing Lisa again made me realize, I no longer loved her. I had said that before, but today, it became an unwavering truth. She had quickly become another face in the montage of those who had, without a care, walked away from a future with me in it.

Though I had moved on, that nagging, incessant thought hung around my neck, like a weight. No matter how I tried to shake it off, it swung back again, pulling me down with it.

That's how life was anyway, wasn't it? My mother's voice filled my thoughts, trying to persuade me otherwise: "In all things God works for the good of those who love him ..." emphasis on *all things*. This day, I supposed, should be included. No way could I have predicted that Pretty Boy—Carter—would recruit my ex to redecorate his house. Especially knowing what I did about the guy's finances.

I exhaled again, my foot pressing harder on the brake, my patience thinning at the length of this red light. I shouldn't have charged out of there. Greta hadn't asked me to stay—nor had she told me ahead of time exactly what Carter had asked of her.

Why did that bug me so much? Did I think that a burger and a kiss somehow entitled me to knowledge of her future plans? How could I when I'd offered—and given—Lisa so much more only to see her walk away as if our engagement had only been a suggestion?

The light turned green, but instead of surging through the traffic, I started off slowly, thinking. Greta did not owe me a thing. Nor had she made any predictions—or promises —about the future.

Perhaps that unspoken truth was what had made Lisa's surprise appearance all the more distasteful. My two worlds —one from the past and the other, emerging—had crossed paths and still, I found myself very much an outsider.

I had reached Harbor Boulevard now, the final stretch before making the turn onto the peninsula I, for better or worse, called home. Perhaps it was the drive that gave me the headspace to realize, once again, that it was all out of my hands.

---

**Greta**

I WANTED to talk to Zac. To ask him deeper, probing questions about Lisa. Why hadn't he mentioned to me that he was thinking of selling the house to her? Did he think I wouldn't be interested to know that?

Or maybe he simply thought it was none of my business.

Though I had tried to avoid any more contact with Lisa earlier today, she'd found me outside on the deck.

"I'll be going now."

"Thanks for letting me know."

"No, thank *you* for allowing me to interrupt your vacation."

I only nodded.

This did nothing to keep her from approaching me, something obviously on her mind. I took the reins. "Is there something more?"

Lisa slid a quick look over her shoulder. "Please don't mention what I told you to Zac. Not before we hash out all the details of the sale."

"Of course."

She hesitated. "See, it's really a matter of urgency that he take me up on my generous offer, well, the one I'm going to make to him very soon."

I doubted this. Then again, to some it might seem a

matter of urgency to ... buy a beach house. But I stayed still, listening.

Lisa lowered her voice. "I'm very concerned about what would happen to Gus and Emily if I don't."

I frowned. "Did you mean Gus and Helen?"

Her eyes widened. "Yes, yes, Helen. That's who I meant. Gus and Helen."

"What is it that you think might happen to them?"

She sighed. "I'm afraid Zac is getting ready to evict them."

I nearly laughed.

She reached out and touched my forearm. "I'm perfectly serious. Carter tells me Zac's been doing all kinds of work in the apartment—"

I shook my head, interrupting her. "To make their lives better."

Lisa gave me a sad little smile. "I wish that were true. Like I said, the man's a workaholic. He's also a penny pincher, and by now I'm sure he's become aware of just how valuable that lockout is. I mean"—she gestured to my rental space—"just look what Carter has here."

Now, hours later, as I sat on the floor of my small bedroom I mulled over Lisa's adamance over buying Zac's house. Once again, I recalled telling Zac how beautiful I thought it was here, only to see him shrug his shoulders. In the short amount of time we had spent together, I had come to believe that he might be experiencing a change of heart. Had my growing feelings for him misinterpreted something?

I rested my back against the side of the bed, shutting out the news, as well as the other bombshell Lisa had dropped on me. Listlessly, I scrolled through photos Clara had sent from her recent visit to our Grandma Violet. Clara's big eyes and curly hair only served to further accentuate the gaunt look in Grams's face. A sad ache caught in my throat. I didn't want to cry. Not while I was so far away from home and could not visit her myself.

For the second time in a day, I had a passing thought to pack up my bag and go home.

I was still holding my phone when it rang, startling me. Not simply because it suddenly began to ring, but because of who was on the other end. Tommy's name blazed across the screen.

How could I have forgotten? In her texts, Clara had mentioned that Tommy had been poking around, asking if I was home. She said that in her haste to get him off the phone, she'd slipped and said that I'd gone on vacation. Thankfully, she had not told him where.

I sighed. Enough time had passed for me to face whatever it was he wanted to say to me.

"Hello?"

"You answered."

I swallowed, hesitating. "Of course."

"That's funny. You wouldn't take my call after you'd taken a pot shot at me and cancelled the wedding."

So much for facing him. There was no mistaking his lingering bitterness, and I sensed myself retreating.

"Clara says you went on vacation." He swore quietly, but I heard the words loud and clear. "Greta, I can't believe you went to Hawaii without me."

Through his anger, I also heard pain. Whatever had transpired between us, I couldn't let him believe that I had taken our honeymoon without him.

"I'm not in Hawaii, Tommy. I canceled that trip, as I told

you I would." Though I had paid for it with my own funds anyway.

"Whatever you say."

I shifted, keenly aware that whatever I said, both in the past and now, he would probably disregard or call me hysterical. Suggest that I lived outside of reality. What was it he used to say?

*Get your head out of la-la land, Greta.*

I cleared my throat. "Tommy, was there something you wanted to tell me?"

"Should there be?"

"Well, I don't know. You, uh, called me."

"Where are you?"

"I'd rather not say."

"So you're hiding from me?"

I frowned. "Of course not."

"Then why not tell me?"

"I'm ... well, I'm in California, if you must know. I learned some interesting information about my, uh, great-grandmother."

"The dead one?"

My face grew cold. "She was once a movie starlet, so I decided to come out here to find out a little more about that, to walk in her shoes, so to speak."

My confession was met with silence. I opened my mouth to explain, but before I could utter another word, he laughed. Hard. He sounded as if he could hardly catch his breath. I waited him out, sorry that I had bothered to tell him as much as I had.

"So you're telling me that you dumped me so you could go all the way out to California on some whim? To walk by

Grauman's Chinese Theater and step over the bums so you could look at all those stars on the sidewalk?"

I clammed up. Why had I thought Tommy would care about what I dreamed about?

"You there, Greta?"

"If you have nothing more to say, Tommy," I said quietly, "then I think we should end this call now."

"Now, hold on a second. You bet I have something to say. Here it is: Have you come to your senses yet?"

"Senses? About ... what?"

"What do you mean, about what? Us, Greta. Us!" He howled a long, groan-filled breath into the phone. "When you told me you were done, I knew better. I stepped back. Gave you your space. But now it's time to talk it out and make a plan."

"Make a ...?" I shook my head. "Tommy, maybe I wasn't clear. I truly thought I was when I said I couldn't marry you."

"It's not what you meant."

I closed my eyes. Had I given him false hope that, some-day, I would change my mind? A twist of guilt seized my heart. A mental picture formed. In my mind, I saw that gift of a framed photo, the one we had received from an anony-mous giver. We had been happy the day that engagement photo had been taken, but beneath our smiles, too many questions remained. If I were to place a bet, something told me Tommy would agree—if only his pride allowed him to.

"It truly is what I meant, Tommy. I'm sorry. If I gave you the impression that I had simply gotten cold feet, or that I was unsure, then I hope you'll forgive me. I can't marry you, Tommy. Not ever."

He sucked in a breath. I could hear it through the phone, plain as if we were sitting right next to one another.

"Then you, Greta, are a ... liar."

I gasped. A flash of heat filled my face. "If you called me to throw out insults, then this call is over."

"You were happy. Tell me you were." His voice faltered a little, catching me off guard. "Say it."

I shook my head, tears welling. I tried to shake them away—I was never an easy crier—but soon hot tears rolled down my face, and my sinuses filled.

"I sent you a picture, Greta, to remind you of how it used to be between us. But you probably had already left."

I froze. "You ... what? Was it a framed picture from our engagement shoot?"

"You saw it?"

"There was no note."

He didn't offer an excuse. I sniffled, sitting up straighter. That out-of-the blue gift, or "reminder" as he called it, had helped me reach the decision to make this trip in the first place. "There was a no return address either."

"Did you like it? The picture, I mean?"

I had been blaming myself for months, guilty torture keeping me up at nights. If only I had followed my inner nigglings and stopped my relationship with Tommy from progressing as far as it had.

But now I realized, it was time to forgive—myself. In Tommy I had seen the possibility of the romantic future I'd always dreamed of but could never quite attain. When it became clear that I had been mistaken, that he was not the one for me, I tried to end it. But Tommy had made that very, very difficult.

"So?" he asked again. "Did you like the gift I sent to the house, Greta?"

Realization burned me—the engagement photo. "You sent that photo to manipulate me."

"I sent it to remind you."

"No. No, you didn't, Tommy." I mustered the courage I needed. "Let me be perfectly clear: Our relationship is over. I will never marry you. Please, Tommy—don't ever call me again."

I hung up, unwilling to give him one more opportunity to play with my emotions. There had already been too much of that today, and I was growing weary of it. I pulled myself up and padded over to the window. From this side of the house, I had a peekaboo of the sea beyond the deck and above that, a wide swath of pinkish blue sky.

I had come here for a purpose as well as a respite, but it was becoming clear that I had lost my focus and allowed the fantasy of a relationship with the boy next door to derail me. My face heated again, thinking about that kiss we shared on the beach in the dark. I'd had a history of missteps where men were concerned, and I sensed that the matriarchs before me could say the same. My conversation with Tommy proved that, perhaps, I was making them still.

How would I ever know what was real and what was not? My insides sank under that question. Truth was, I had little hope of my relationship with Zac growing into anything long lasting. How could it in such a short time when we both still faced demons from our pasts? Something told me Zac knew this too.

I watched the sky turn from blues to shades of pinks to fiery reds.

*Who were you, 'R'? And what did you mean to my great-gran?*

I had to stop allowing the fantasy of happily-ever-after from getting in the way of searching for a long-ago link to my family's past—elusive as that may be.

# CHAPTER SIXTEEN

**ZAC**

Living a life preoccupied with tissue samples and their transformation, the curiosity of it all driving me to long hours of study and contemplation, had made me realize one thing: I had developed an uncanny ability to block out everything else. In this case, Greta. I hadn't called her last night, nor had she contacted me. My gut was in knots.

Without work to keep me consumed, I'd had to find something else to help me practice avoidance. To prove my point, I nimbly poured a second cup of coffee and looked through the pile of mail that had collected on the kitchen countertop. Sport peered at me from her post on the couch. Even she sensed the tension in this place.

My phone rang, and without thinking it through, I picked it up.

"Oh, good, Zacky, it's you." Lisa had apparently reverted to her pet name for me. I hated it.

"Lisa."

"Aw, I recognize that voice. You haven't had your morning coffee, have you."

To answer her, I slurped into the phone.

Lisa laughed loudly, the sound of it like the high-pitched whir of a power drill. I poured my leftover coffee into the sink and tossed the mug in behind it. A twinge of rogue guilt twisted in my chest. I hadn't spoken to Greta since Lisa showed up at her place yesterday, and that fact become further illuminated by this surprise call.

"I'm honored that you chose to answer my call this morning, Zacky." Her voice had turned soft. I knew she wanted something. Didn't mean I had license to be a jerk, though.

"What is it, Lisa?"

"First, how's my dog?"

I snapped a look at Sport. Her eyes slid a glance toward me, and one of her ears twitched, but otherwise, she was unmoved.

"Sport's doing great. Never better."

"Sport! That's a, a terrible name for my sweet Bubbles."

I rolled my eyes, like a sullen teen. If I didn't stay on my guard, a surly attitude would stick with me all day. I threw open the slider door to my front deck, a sudden urge to get some sun and salt on me.

I hadn't expected a blast of cool air to greet me too. Sport followed me outside long enough to get some wind in her fur. Then she turned tail and trotted back inside.

"What was it you wanted to talk about?" I asked.

"Let's meet for lunch. My treat!"

I leaned onto the deck railing, allowing a deep stretch to work out the tension knotting through my back. "Can't. Sorry."

"See? Now this is why I worry about you. Always working. Never taking time off." She tsked. "It's not healthy."

"I appreciate the concern, but at this moment, I'm letting the sun's rays beat down on me, and I've got the sound of waves to keep me company. I'd say, I'm doing all right."

"I thought you hated the beach."

"Whatever gave you that idea?"

She seemed to hesitate at this. "What do you mean? *You* gave me that idea! May I remind you that you said you wished you'd never bought that money pit!"

I twisted my mouth. Probably had said something to that effect, especially after I'd put my savings into the place only to have her change her mind about marrying me.

A chill ran through me. If she hadn't ended things, we would likely be married right now. I stole a glance next door. Greta's deck stood empty.

I landed a fist of resolve onto the railing. "If there's nothing else, Lisa, then I'll say goodbye now."

"There is something else: I want the house."

"Come again?"

I could hear her inhaling harshly, perhaps revving up to state her case. "I said I want the house. I will pay you fairly for it."

I shook my head, confused by her sudden announcement. Unless this had been her plan all along? Hadn't I already learned that Lisa had trouble with telling the truth?

"What makes you think that I would want to sell the house, Lisa?" I paused. "Well, other than that misunderstanding over my thoughts on the beach, that is."

"Think about it, Zacky. *I'm* the one who wanted the house in the first place. *I* talked *you* into it. I had offered to move in there while all the work was being done, but you insisted that you could handle it. I appreciate that, Zac, but it's time for me to take it all off of your hands. No sense arguing over it." She laughed. "You know I'm right."

I let my silence on the line do the talking. Then I hauled in a deep breath, planted my feet wide, and surveyed my slice of the neighborhood. Some of the houses on the ocean side lacked character. Some were falling apart. Still others, like the one I was living in right now, burst with people who loved everything about living in this mismatch of houses built on tiny lots. And I had no intention of leaving anytime soon.

"I'm sorry, Lisa. My answer is no."

"Excuse me? Surely you don't mean that?"

I kept my voice steady, calm, unwilling to beat this subject over and over. Yet, it was important that I made myself clear.

"I absolutely do mean it, Lisa. But let me say this: You are correct about one thing. I may not have been keen on this move in the beginning, but it has turned out to be the right choice for me. I suppose I have you to thank for that."

"I cannot believe what I'm hearing!" There was no trace left of that that happy-go-lucky, sing-song voice she had used at the start of this conversation. "This isn't over, Zac. I promise you that!"

I briefly shut my eyes, slightly put out that my attempt at smoothing things over by showing my gratitude to her was met with such contempt. You win some, you ... well, this was a loss I was willing to let go.

"Goodbye, Lisa. I hope"—I hesitated, sensing sarcasm rising. I tamped it down, replacing it with the kind of grace I didn't deserve but always desired—"I hope all goes well with you and that you have a beautiful future."

She clicked off the line so quickly that I wasn't sure if she had heard the last few words I'd said. Probably didn't matter much anyway. I'd half-expected Lisa to ask me to take her back. Wouldn't have happened. I know now how wrong we were for each other. Still, it would have been nice to be asked, rather than the shakedown I'd just endured.

Back inside, I found my sneakers and put them on while Sport sniffed around my feet. Already, the day had been full. Or so it felt.

I plopped down next to Sport, allowing her to climb into my lap. Nothing like a furry beast to tame the stress right out of a person. I chuckled ruefully. My father used to say that and now I caught myself repeating it. Oddly, I was never all that enamored with animals when I was a kid. Books had been my hobby. And getting into trouble with Brax. This was all very new.

Sport headbutted my hand, and I realized I'd stopped petting her. "Sorry about that." I grinned at the beast. Hadn't done this much of *nothing much*, in a very long time. "Guess you caught me riding down Memory Lane."

I gave her one more quick rub between her ears, scooped her up, then headed out back to the wasteland also known as my backyard. I glanced around the entire narrow garden-less backyard. For as small as this space was, it held a lot of ... stuff. I put Sport back down, found some gloves, and began picking through the pile of castoffs that I had been storing out here until, well, *mañana*.

I was well into the busy work before hearing voices conversing. One, in particular, caught me by the throat. Greta. She and Gus were having what sounded like an animated conversation inside the apartment.

Sport ran over and jumped up, planting a nudge on my

face. "Knock it off." I laughed and pushed her away, then dried my cheek with the side of my upper arm. She did it again but jumped higher this time.

"You trying to tell me something?"

She tilted a look at me that said, "Ya think?"

I groaned. "Fine. I hear her too, you know."

Sport's mouth opened, and her tongue dangled out. Her eyes went on alert.

"Give me a sec, will you?"

She whined.

I filled up a waste barrel on the side of the house, cramming every crevice with debris, debris I should have managed better.

Gus's familiar voice slipped out through an open window. "So this fella wanted you back."

"I'm afraid so," Greta was saying.

"And you told him no."

"I absolutely did. Oh, Gus, you should have heard him. First he sounded sad, then angry. My emotions were all over the place."

I closed the lid quietly, my hands and arms filthy. Sport pawed me on the leg, but I shushed her. Her eyes seemed to darken, as if she was on to my eavesdropping. I screwed up my mouth. It wasn't like I *intended* to listen.

"Well, honey, it's no big surprise to me. That boy knew he'd made a terrible mistake leaving you like that. Yessiree, I'm only surprised it took him this long to figure that out."

"But it wasn't like that—"

"He isn't worth defending, Greta."

"He wasn't right for me, Gus. I've finally come to terms with that, but here's the thing—*I* was the one who ended things between us."

"I know, I know, you said that's what you told him, and I support your decision one-hundred-percent!"

Greta replied in a soft voice. "No, I mean, I'm the one who called off the wedding in the first place."

I froze in place and quickly became incapable of reacting to Sport's near-frantic clawing on my leg. A knife-like pain twisted in my stomach.

I searched my mind. What had she told me about her heartbreak? I pushed hard to remember, but it was no use. I'd had every reason to believe that she had been the one left hurt and abandoned. Maybe she had not told me specifically, but I had witnessed some of the aftermath of that broken heart. Bottom line: Greta had led me to believe that she had been dumped.

Like *I* had been dumped.

I jammed my tongue into the side of my cheek, trying to force off the dread of disappointment that bulldozed its way right through me. Oh, I wasn't disappointed that Greta hadn't been hurt by the guy—I wouldn't wish that on her. Ever.

What *had* cut me to my core was that she had, by omitting an important fact, not told me the truth. My gut clenched, reminders of Lisa filling my head.

I paused, pushing away the sense that I was being ... irrational. Greta probably had plenty of good reasons for letting the guy go. Of course, I couldn't pretend that I wasn't glad she was no longer with him.

Still, why had she not mentioned what had really happened? Especially in light of Carter's comment on that first day that she had been—what did he say?—left at the altar.

I stifled a groan, my head wagging, as if I'd heard some unexpected news.

Didn't matter now anyway. She was leaving, something that the women in my life tended to do. The truth of that realization tamped down any notion of a future that I may have been entertaining.

I backed away from the window and motioned for Sport to follow. In my brain, I knew fear had begun to control me. All I could do now was not allow another woman to become close enough to give those fears anymore power.

---

## Greta

Gus's sweet face looked back at me as I spilled my heart out over the call I received from Tommy last night. Lucky for Helen that she had taken an Uber to visit her sister in an assisted living center one town over. She hadn't had to listen to me go on and on.

Not that I meant to take my problems to him. I'd been on my way out for a walk along the water's edge, knowing the gentle curl of waves would soothe my knot of worries. As I passed by his window, though, Gus called out to me. I jumped, my thoughts still so muddled. And reluctantly, I wandered inside.

"What's got you all tangled up?" he'd asked.

I tried to give him a clichéd answer, but he kept pressing.

"Go on now. I know when a girl's upset about something."

It had occurred to me I'd never had a man in my life like

Gus, hadn't ever divulged personal information to a father-like figure before. For some reason, I wanted to do that now, to tell him about the call and, well, probably more than he cared to hear.

I didn't regret it. There was no judgment in Gus's face, especially as I told him that it was I, not Tommy, who had ended things.

"Greta," he finally said, "you are a smart girl, and you had your reasons."

"So that's why his call was so ... difficult," I told him. "Well, that and what he said about my reason for coming out here in the first place." I found myself sighing more lately. "He made all kinds of fun of that."

"Now, go on. See? The guy's showing you that you made the right call, all right!"

"You are a sweet, sweet man, Mr. Gus."

He gave me a garbled laugh at that. "Mr. Gus!"

"You've listened to me long enough. Now that I'm here, what can I do for you? Are you hungry?"

"Well, I don't know. Can you cook?"

"I won't be opening any restaurants, but I can hold my own in the kitchen." I patted my stomach. "Evidenced by this."

"You're as skinny as a rail!"

I laughed and bounded toward the door. "Tell you what. I'll run next door to my place and make you a sandwich. I promise to deliver it to you as fast as possible. You won't starve while I'm gone, will you?"

"I'll try not to, missy!"

I took the stairs two at a time, astonished that my limited cooking skills were being used to feed two men in as many days. Clara would be so proud.

Within a few minutes, my kitchen counter looked much like it did yesterday, only with the addition of plastic containers with lids that were kept in a bottom cabinet. I grabbed both containers brimming with lunches and jogged back down the stairs.

Zac was waiting for me at the bottom. He looked ... dirty, his arms and hands reminiscent of mine after a morning of digging in the garden.

"Zac?"

"Greta."

There was steel in his gaze. I held up the containers. "I'm on my way over to Gus's. Did you, uh, need something?"

His eyes flickered. I half expected him to break out his high-wattage smile, but he stuck one hand against his hip in a way that corrected me. Something was bothering him.

I swallowed, waiting for his response. I still had questions for him related to Lisa but hadn't exactly meted out how to bring it all up. Especially since it wasn't really any of my business. Well, at least the part about him selling his house to her.

Plus, Lisa had asked me not to mention it until she'd spoken to him. Had she done that? Could this explain the guarded expression?

His jaw tightened. "What happened with your wedding?"

"What?"

"What ... happened?"

"I-I, well, we broke up." I tilted my head, unsure of where this line of questioning was coming from. "I'm pretty sure I told you that already, right?"

"How?"

"How *what*?"

"How did it break up? What happened?"

Everything about this confrontation felt awkward and out of place. I should have been the one demanding answers. Not him.

"Be honest with me," he continued.

I narrowed my eyes, my rankles up. Talking about my failed engagement had, overnight, become the topic du jour. Finally, I said, "I called it off."

His eyes flickered, and he licked his lips, his voice barely above a whisper. "At least you told the truth this time."

"Excuse me?"

He looked away briefly. "Nothing."

"No, not nothing." I shifted the sandwiches to my other hand and lifted my gaze to meet his. "Zac, why would you think I lied to you?"

He didn't break eye contact. "You told me you were heartbroken over the end of your engagement, making it appear that you were the victim."

Victim?

"But I just overheard you tell Gus that you were the one who ended it."

I squinted at him. "Wait a second. You heard me telling Gus? When was ..." My eyes popped open. "Zac, were you spying on me?"

"Not on purpose."

I laughed, reflexively, only it didn't sound all that happy. "Well, it wasn't like I was inside Gus's apartment shouting at him. Zac, you were eavesdropping."

He shifted. "We will have to agree to disagree on that."

"I'm not agreeing."

He stared me down. "Let me ask you, Greta. What did the poor sucker do to make you call it quits? Wine and dine you? Shape his life around yours? Handle your honey-do list twenty-four-seven?"

"Stop it."

"Because in my experience, none of that care and concern matters. They leave anyway."

For a split second, my heart tore for him, and I wanted to reach out and tell Zac that not all women do that.

But too much had happened in the past twenty-four hours, not the least of which all that he had accused me of. How dare he call me a liar? He didn't use that word exactly, but he intimated that I had been withholding the truth, for whatever reason, I didn't know.

And that was enough for me.

"So, you're saying that you would prefer it if *I* had been dumped."

"I'd prefer you had told me the truth."

"Why? So you could be the one to pick up the pieces? To be the hero in my story?"

"It's not about me—I was talking about you."

"I don't think you were, Zac. You're talking about you and Lisa. And yet somehow, I'm the villain."

"You don't know anything about me and Lisa."

"I know that you're a workaholic. You told me yourself that this is the first vacation you've taken in three years. How in the world could you pay decent attention to the woman that you're wooing when you're never there?"

His face flushed. "Not fair."

"I also know that you're incredibly intense, which can make for difficulty in communicating with your partner."

"So that's what you think."

I shook my head and looked out to where the sand beckoned, giving Zac more time to fume.

"You spend one afternoon with Lisa—one *portion* of an afternoon—and suddenly you have me all figured out."

I swung a look back to him. "And you would rather see me dumped by my ex than make a grownup decision to leave a bad relationship!"

He scoffed. "Is that what you think Lisa did? Made a grown up"—he gestured with air quotes—"decision when she decided that, after all the hoops I'd jumped through for her, I wasn't enough?"

"Maybe that was the problem, Zac. Maybe you thought working day and night to buy Lisa everything she asked for was enough. When maybe all she really wanted was ... you."

Silence fell between us like a thud: abrupt and uncomfortable. He climbed up two more stairs until we were a breath away from each other. I began to lose myself in the moment, in the closeness of him. This is what always got me in trouble.

He brushed his gaze over my face. "And what is it *you* want, Greta?"

The deep timbre of his voice made my knees weak. I could fall into the fire of his eyes, conflicted as they were. He made me want to forget about all the angry words we'd swapped and the questions I had yet to pose.

He leaned closer, which was barely possible, his voice a whisper now. "That's what I thought. You have no idea what you want."

As if we hadn't shared an incredibly intimate moment, Zac turned, abruptly, and jumped to the ground from three steps up. I watched him stalk over to his house, climb the stairs, and never look back.

# CHAPTER SEVENTEEN

**GRETA**

I HUNG UP, conflicted. The chance to start fresh had just landed in my life, with no warning.

"We'd like to offer you the executive director position." Judith was the Human Resources Director at Jupiter Events. I'd met her before, briefly. "We'll include a nice upgrade in pay."

I had kept my phone off since yesterday, and the first call that had come in was a job offer. The new owner of Jupiter Events had realized that, without my contacts and skills, the company would struggle. Judith had said as much. I mulled the surprise offer as I stood out here on the beach, watching waves roll onto wet sand.

My cellphone rang, and I answered it.

"I've been trying to reach you all day." Clara sounded agitated.

"I'm so sorry." I exhaled. "I saw you calling and couldn't

grab it on time, but I was in the middle of something anyway, and then I forgot my phone—"

"I need you to come home."

"What? Why?" Sea water pooled around my feet. I had come out to the water's edge to think. "It's Grams, isn't it."

"If you'd let me get a word in edgewise, I could tell you."

"Sorry."

"But you're right." She paused, and I heard what sounded like muffled sniffling. "I was over there again today, and, well, the caregivers there don't think she has much longer, Greta."

I gasped.

"Will you come?"

"Of course, hon." The incoming tide splashed onto my shins, dousing my body with water, but I didn't move. "I'll be there tomorrow."

---

## Greta

AFTER TALKING with my sis a little while longer on the beach, I found a dry spot in the sand and searched for a flight on my phone. With that booked, I lingered there, the lapping of waves soothing my very raw and jagged nerves.

Finally I gathered my courage and called the assisted living center where grandmother lived.

"I'd like to speak to my grandmother, Violet Luna. Is there someone who could assist me?"

With a nurse's help, I heard my Grandmother's familiar

voice. A very real mix of comfort and dread threaded my insides.

"Hi, sweetheart."

Tears flooded my eyes. "I wanted you to know that I'm coming to see you tomorrow." I didn't ask, *please wait for me*.

"I'll be here, darling."

"Promise?"

"Oh, yes.

After a few moments, I hung up, satisfied by the strength in her voice. There was still time. I could feel it.

The next few hours flew by with details, beginning with a call to Carter. When I told him I was leaving, he urged me to return before my lease was up. Said he would leave the light on for me, then he laughed saying that was from an old Motel 6 commercial.

"Something tells me you'll be back," he said. "The end of summer is the best time here, and you won't want to miss it. Trust me."

I smiled slightly at that, while still doubting my return.

That call down, I made my way back outside to say one more "so long" to Gus and Helen, the rush of the ocean causing me to falter. I swallowed back emotion. I wasn't prepared to say goodbye so soon to this little hamlet where my great-grandmother surely once walked—and to the people who made me feel so very welcome.

I held onto the deck rail at the top of the stairs and slid a glance across the divide to Zac's home. Regret seared me, though I tried to blink it away. He and I had ended things poorly. I knew I should say goodbye to him as well, but would he even care? Shut the door in my face? Tell me good riddance?

The piercing call of an alarm broke the melancholy of

the sea's roar. It sounded ... I took a couple of steps down the stairway. It sounded like it was coming from Gus and Helen's. Zac must have realized at the same time because, as I flew toward their front door, he was hustling down his stairs.

I reached them first and tried the door. Locked.

Zac ran over to the side window and cupped his hands around his eyes to see inside. "No smoke that I can tell." He moved to the front door and pounded on it. "Gus! Helen!"

"Don't you have your key?"

"Forgot it upstairs." He pounded again on the door. "Gus! Helen!"

"I'm calling the fire department."

He nodded grimly and turned to run back upstairs. "I'll get the key!"

The side window shot open, and Helen called out, "What's all that racket out there?"

Zac spun back around and jogged back over. "Helen? The fire alarm's going off. Do you hear it?"

A slow kind of realization came over her. "Drat! I think I left beans on the stove." She disappeared in a hurry.

"Open the door," Zac shouted.

We both moved to the door, waiting patiently, saying nothing to each other, both clearly agitated.

Door open, Zac flew inside and over to the stove. I opened a second window and switched on the overhead fan. "Where's Gus?" I asked her over that piercing alarm.

"Heh?"

"Gus," I shouted. "Where is Gus?"

Helen batted a hand at me. "Oh, he's nappin'. Could sleep through a tsunami!"

As the small space filled with fresh air, the smoke alarm

stopped, but the tension in my shoulders remained. Zac re-entered the main room after removing the smoky beans from the stove. His jaw was set, similar to the way it was yesterday, when we'd had a war I'd rather not think about right now.

Helen sneezed. "Excuse me! Must be all that air comin' in here with those windows open."

Zac and I shared a silent glance.

"Helen, I'm going to clean out that pan for you and make sure your alarms are reset. You should leave the windows open until all the smoke dissipates."

She patted his arm. "You take such good care of us."

When he'd left to secure the apartment, I said, "Helen, I was hoping to talk to you and Gus tonight."

"I'm sorry, Greta, but by the time that old Gus gets up, it'll be the middle of the night. Can you talk to him in the mornin'?"

I drew in a deep breath, nearly gagging on the smoke that lingered. "Unfortunately, I'll be gone by then. I have to leave. It's my ... grandmother."

"Oh, no, is she sick?"

"Yes, very." I worked to control the hitch in my voice. "She may not make it much longer."

Helen put her hand to her mouth briefly. "When do you leave?"

"I'll be up with the roosters."

"That early, eh?"

I smiled. "It's the only way I can make it back home during visiting hours." I took her hands in mine. "I just wanted to say goodbye and to tell you both how much I've enjoyed getting to know you and ..."

Before I could say another word, Helen drew me close

and wrapped her thick arms around me. The tears I'd been fighting began to trickle out, and she hugged me tighter still.

When I pulled back, she held onto me. At first I thought she might need her cane, but then I realized, she had something to say. "You have been the dearest blessing to us, Greta. Now don't you blubber anymore and say things like goodbye. You'll be back. I can feel it."

I smiled, hoping I'd find my way back here before summer's end. But doubt nagged at me. We'd suffered loss, Clara and I, more than once, but though I knew our grandmother had been ailing for some time, I had not allowed myself to think of our lives without her in it. I couldn't, even now.

Zac reappeared in the living area, his face a mask. It was as if I weren't even in the room. "I think you're safe to close up all the windows now, Helen. Do you have something else to eat tonight?"

"Yes, yes, we're fine. Go on now, you two. You've done enough for us for one day."

I hugged her once more and slipped out the door, vaguely aware of Zac behind me. I crossed the divide between our houses and landed on the bottom step, when I heard him call my name.

I looked back over my shoulder at him. "Yes?"

His expression was sober. "May I come up?"

Slowly, I shrugged, gestured toward the stairs with a flick of my head and headed back up with him following behind.

Inside my apartment, I headed toward the fridge. It dawned on me that I could offer the remaining food to Zac. But then I thought better of it and decided to tell Carter to come and take it. I grabbed two bottles of Perrier and spun around.

"Thirsty?"

He reached for a bottle but didn't drink it. "Were you going to tell me you were leaving?"

I opened my bottle, took a long, burning sip, my eyes focused on him. I replaced the cap and set the bottle on the counter. "How did you know?"

"I overheard you tell Helen."

I put my hand on my hip. "You're making a habit of eavesdropping."

He pursed his lips. "You weren't planning to say goodbye."

"I wasn't sure."

"Why?"

The flash of pain in his eyes made me ask myself the same. For a brief moment, our confrontation dissipated, as had my questions about Lisa buying his house or anything else she'd said about him.

He dropped his crossed arms. "You have every right to make your own decision."

"Yes, I do." I reached out for the counter, as if to use it for stability. "My grandmother's not doing well, Zac. I'm leaving to be with her. It's as simple as that."

That tense lift of his shoulders dropped some. He nodded. "I'm sorry, Greta. Is there anything I can do?"

I waved my hand in the air, as if to say *no, there's absolutely nothing you can do.* But I stopped myself. "You can pray for her. And for me."

"You got it."

"Thank you."

He shifted. "When will you be back?"

"I'm not sure if I will be. I-I also have a job interview—a

formality, really. A promotion with the company that bought us out."

"Oh," He seemed to lose focus, like he'd taken a football to the gut. Eventually, he said, "I hadn't heard. Will you be taking it?"

I shrugged.

He pressed his lips together a moment, presumably weighing my non-committal response. "I was going to find you tonight, you know," he said. "To apologize."

"For calling me a liar?"

Frustration crossed his face. "I didn't use that word."

"It's what you meant."

He ran a hand through his hair, as if frustrated. "I'm sorry for getting so heated, for not listening to you, for assuming things I should not have."

"You've been busy."

He groaned. "I'm sorry, Greta."

He looked so forlorn and sincere that I wanted to rush to him and pull him into my arms. But there was still too much unspoken, so I simply said, "I forgive you."

We stood there silent, space between us. It wasn't awkward, exactly, but I began to wonder if we should stop there and consider a truce. Our second truce since we met.

"Lisa called me."

"Did she now?"

"She had some crazy idea that I would sell her the house." He rubbed the side of his neck repeatedly, as if to erase the memory. "I told her no."

"You did? I thought you didn't really like the beach all that much."

"I have had a change of heart."

I nodded. "Well, I didn't think you were going to sell it to her anyway."

He coughed a laugh. "You knew about this?"

"She mentioned she was going to make you an offer. Said you were always unhappy here and that she had come into some money. I believe she said she'd be doing you a favor."

"Oh brother. How did you know she was bluffing?"

I shrugged. "At first, I didn't. I was pretty taken aback to hear her plan, didn't really care to hear it. She kept talking anyway."

"She does that."

"Yes, well, then she began telling me about how she roped you into buying this place. That it had been a dump. I remembered you saying that you worked all the time, barely got outside to see that green flash—I haven't seen it yet, by the way." I pushed myself away from the counter and stepped closer to him. "And it all suddenly made sense. With that kind of schedule, you could live anywhere. Maybe her plan would work."

"I'm confused. I thought you said you didn't think I was going to sell it to her."

I ignored that. "Is it true that the house belonged to Gus and Helen originally?"

He furrowed his brow. "It did. Out of respect for them, though, I never mentioned it. You've been getting so close to them, I figured it would come up sometime anyway. It's their story to tell."

"Hm."

"What hm?"

"Right. She also said something else. That you were planning to kick them out of the apartment soon."

His jaw set. "Did she say why?"

"For one thing, you'd be able to rent the apartment for a *lot* more money."

"Yeah, because I've always been all about money."

"She told me that she'd had to talk you into letting them stay in the first place."

Zac stepped closer to me now. He pressed a fist into the counter and looked directly at me "You really believed her?"

I rolled my eyes. "Pfsst. No."

He looked relieved, if not a little confused. "Why?"

I came around the island, too, a muddle of confusion myself. Still, I knew what I knew. "She was pretty convincing, but I've seen your character in action, Zac. What she said didn't fit the you I've come to know."

He took another step toward me. "You know me, huh?"

I shrugged a little. "I think I do."

Tentatively, Zac touched my face. He looped a stray hair around my ear, never taking his eyes off me. "Thank you for not believing that garbage Lisa spewed. I wouldn't have blamed you if you had."

I shook my head. "The more I thought about it, the charges she was making about you, the angrier I became."

"More angry than you were at me the other night?"

I smiled ruefully. "I just didn't show it quite so much. Zac, I do think you should watch out for Lisa. I'm not convinced she will let up."

"I'm not worried."

"Yeah, didn't think you would be."

He speared me with a look. "I don't want to talk about Lisa anymore."

"Agreed." I stepped back but he caught me gently by the wrist. "I should finish packing."

"About that," he said, his voice turning husky. "Promise me you'll be back."

I hesitated. "I don't think I can."

"Because of your grandmother?"

"That and the job and ... I have some things to work on."

He gave me a sad smile and touched my cheek lightly. "Don't we all? Greta, we don't have to wait for you to return. Let's make a promise to each other now, before you leave, to see where what's between us might lead."

I'd always been drawn to romance, the shining knight kind that curls a girl's toes with one glance. Though I would have denied it at the time, my coming here was some kind of fantasy to play out. I wanted to walk where my great-grandmother had and I had accomplished that, hadn't I?

I had realized something else, though. Life was not one long vacation. It was hard work. Caring for family. Faith. And figuring out who you are in the midst of a world full of hurt people making mistakes that hurt others. I was tired of making mistakes, especially when it came to men, as my mom had done, and as far as I could tell, my great-grandmother before her.

I had come close to adding to the chain of missteps with my engagement to Tommy, but the mistakes had to end with me.

"I'm sorry," I told him, my heart still very unsure. "I don't think I'm ready for it to lead anywhere."

———

DEAREST MOTHER,

. . .

I PRAY that this letter finds you well. I am sorry that I have not written in many days. I am very confused by the turn my time here has taken. I sit for long days on the sand with nary a chance to be in front of the camera.

Mr. Melford has found another girl to be a stand in for Agnes. What did I do wrong, I wonder?

When I asked Anna-Rose what she thought, she said I should stay quiet. She said Mr. Valentino might not be too pleased at my downcast face.

I used the acting skills which I have gained to smile when I do not feel happy at all. My heart ached as I watched Mr. Winston and Mr. Melford frame a scene with a different girl standing in for Miss Ayres.

Please say a prayer for me.


LIZZIE

# CHAPTER EIGHTEEN

## GRETA

IT DID NOT MATTER how absorbing the in-flight magazine might be, nothing distracted more than turbulence at thirty-thousand feet. In the past four and a half hours, the other passengers and I experienced that more times than I cared to think about. No sense going *there*.

What had pulled my attention away from the unthinkable was the freshly offered decision for me. In the land of uncertainty, I could use something sure and stable. From what I had been told, the position at Jupiter Events sounded like that and more. With Clara's writing career tied to her ability—or inability—to bring in consistent money, as recent history had shown, one of us had to have certain work.

We were fairly close to home, the plane's drone steadier than it had been for hours. I laid my head against my seat back and practiced breathing deeply. Would it be so bad if life continued on in this way? Clara had a career of sorts, and now I would have a job earning regular income. We owned the family home, and over time, had made it quite comfortable.

My eyes lulled. Maybe we needed a pet or two to round out the family. I yawned into my fist. Hadn't Clara said something about a cat? I was more of a dog person, but a cat would do. Yes, that's what we'd do—live happily ever after, my sister and me ... and our cat.

Hardly any time had passed before I awoke to the harshness of overhead lighting and buckles being unbuckled. I deplaned in a fog, stopped at the restroom, and then took a cab straight to Grams's assisted living center. I'd texted Clara that I was on my way, and she promised to meet me there.

The receptionist didn't question it when I showed up dragging my suitcase behind me. The staff was probably used to visitors arriving in a hurry. I found my way to Grams's room, pausing only to take a deep, energizing breath, and then walked inside.

To my surprise, she was sitting up. My heart skipped.

"Darling!" she said.

I gave Clara, who was sitting in a chair on the other side of the bed, a guarded look. Then I bent to give Grams a kiss on the cheek. Overcome, I leaned in to hug her neck.

After pulling a chair up next to the bed, I took hold of her hand. "It is good to see you, Grams."

"It is always good to see you, dear. But tell me, did you not have time for a shower today?"

I gasped. Clara laughed silently. I could tell by the way her shoulders bounced. "What do you mean?"

Grams swung a conspiratorial look at Clara before returning her gaze to me. "You are a bit untidy."

I leaned back, aghast.

Clara was laughing uproariously.

"I assure you I showered early this morning. I'm sorry I'm not put together a little better, but I've been on a plane for hours, and then I rushed right over here to see you." I was breathless, so I slowed down. "Forgive me?"

"You were on a *plane?*"

Clara cut in. "Don't you remember? I told you Greta went to California. Now do you remember?"

Grams looked from Clara, then to me. "Was my mother there?"

My heart sank. She was so mixed up. I reached for her hand again, but she pulled it away and began to laugh with more energy than I thought a woman in her condition would have. "I was teasing! Oh, Greta, the look on your face!"

The fact that I had hardly eaten or slept all day was quickly catching up with me. I sat back in the chair, like the crumpled mess I felt.

"Oh dear, I've upset you. I know! Let's play double solitaire. Shall we?" She turned to Clara. "Get me my cards, Clara, will you? And I will need my glasses too."

I peeled a look at Clara, realization dawning on me. "Grams." I turned to her. "Would you excuse Clara and me for a moment?"

Grams looked solemn. "Yes, of course. Now would be a good time for that shower dear."

I gave her a feeble smile, caught Clara's attention and flicked my head toward the door. When we were out of earshot, I grabbed my fiction-writing sister by the sleeve.

"What in the world, Clara?" I hissed. "Grams seems perfectly fine to me."

"Would you rather she be ill?"

"You told me she was ... that she wouldn't make it too much longer."

"I mean, really, how do you quantify 'too much longer'?"

"Clara!"

She shushed me and looked around. "All right, all right. She really did have a couple of bad nights this week and, well, one of the nurses mentioned that she was worried. I just thought you should know. How was I supposed to know that she'd snap out of it?"

Unbelievable! "Snap ... snap out of it? Clara, you scared me to death. Not to mention you wrecked my vacation." I hadn't mentioned the job offer that had been dangled in front of me like one very large carrot. Wasn't the point.

"More like sabbatical."

"What do you mean?"

"Nothing really, it's just, you've been gone so long already, far longer than normal people take vacation."

"You knew all about my trek to California. You encouraged it!"

Clara looked deflated. She let out an exaggerated sigh. "I know that."

"If Grams is doing as well as can be expected, why did you have me fly all the way here? It cost me a fortune."

She shrugged one shoulder half-heartedly. "You can afford it since you're one of those no-debt weirdos."

I stared her down.

She gave an exasperated little look to the ceiling. "I have writer's block."

"I don't understand."

"I can't do it, Greta. I can't write without you here."

I narrowed my eyes at her. "Tell me you're kidding."

"Think about my titles, Greta: *Her First Love, The Boyfriend's Second Chance, A Cowboy's Dilemma—*"

"I'm not listening to this."

"*Her Best Blind Date! A Secret Love—*"

I grabbed Clara's hands, attempting to shut her up.

"They represent all the guys you've dated. You've inspired every one of my books, dear sister. Without my muse, I'm nothing. All washed up!"

"Overly dramatic." I let her hands go roughly, unable to believe my sister would go to these lengths. I set my chin. "I'm going to use the restroom now and try to make myself more presentable for our grandmother."

Clara started to laugh, but I quelled her outburst with a look.

"Then I'm going to go in there and let her beat me at solitaire," I said, 'but I assure you, this isn't over."

Clara nodded, all trace of a smile erased. She held up a key. "I'm going to take a cab. Give you time alone with her"— she gestured toward Grams's door—"and a little more time away from me. You can take my car."

I snatched the key from her and didn't bother saying goodbye when she left, her writerly tail between her legs.

Minutes later I returned to find Grams dozing, her glasses still on her nose. Quietly, I walked to the other side and sat in the chair Clara had vacated. I noticed her Bible sitting on the nightstand and reached for it. When I did, a folded slip of paper fell out. The letter Clara had told me about.

A sleepy voice said, "That was my mama's letter."

"Hm. And you've kept it all these years."

"Mm. Yes. She kept them in a box." Grams yawned, the

fatigue in her eyes more real to me now than when I had walked in earlier.

"May I ask why you've kept it with you?"

She smiled it me now, her head still leaning back against her pillow. "It's a reminder to me to pray, pray, pray." She yawned again. "I failed my daughter, but I won't fail you and your sister."

"Grams, whatever does that mean?"

Her eyes filled with sleep. "My, I'm tired."

I leaned over and felt her cheek. "I should let you rest."

"No, no. I very much want to tell you, darling, that I pray for you and for Clara, that you would not have the sins of the past visited on you." She sighed and attempted to sit up. She fell back against her pillow. "I failed your mother in that way."

"Don't say that."

"It's true. I didn't pray for her as I should have, and she chose ..."

"My father."

Grams nodded. "But the Lord blessed us all with you and with Clara. Despite our wrong choices, His love for us knows no bounds!"

The tension of the past twenty-four hours began to melt. I kissed Grams on the cheek. "You never failed Mom. I assure you."

She smiled, though I sensed sadness around the edges.

I tilted my head to one side, intrigued by the letter that she had been using for a bookmark for who-knew-how-long. I did not want to tell her that I knew the contents of it, but I dearly wanted an up-close look. "May I open it?"

"Yes, darling."

I unfolded the letter carefully, reveling in the penmanship, not to mention the longing in the words. I took another look at Grams. Today she was clear minded, lucid, but many times, this was not the case. I was struck by how it had not occurred to either Clara or me that she would have any knowledge of "R's" identity. Had we even bothered to show her the postcard from long ago?

My heart began to beat rapidly. "Grams, I have to ask you something."

"Yes?"

"Do you know who 'R' was?"

I tensed, ready to learn that our great-grandmother had, indeed, once been in love with the one and only Rudolph Valentino.

"Why, yes, I believe I do remember. It was ... wait just a second. Oh, my mind slips at the worst times. May I see it again?"

I handed the letter to her, and after several seconds of quiet study, she smiled. "It's Anna-Rose, but my mother called her Rose."

How ... how could that be? "I don't understand. I thought the letter writer was a man, and that he was writing to Great-gran, asking her to come back to him."

She peered at me, an amused expression on her face. "I thought Clara was the writer."

I cracked a smile, though my fantasy was rapidly fading. "Are you sure about the letter writer's identity?"

She dropped her arm to her side, still holding the letter. "She was a friend of my mother's and dearly wanted her to return to California. But your great-grandmother had a good head on her shoulders—you probably don't know that phrase. It means she had a strong will and mind. But it was more than that."

I waited, expectantly.

"She also had found love."

"In California?"

"No, right here in Indiana. With my father."

---

"Anna-Rose?!"

Clara's facial expression looked as incredulous as I felt. "From what I gathered, Anna-Rose was a friend of Great-gran's."

"Wow." Clara shook her head. "I never saw that coming."

"So much for chasing Valentino, hm?"

Clara looked up from her child's pose on the floor. I often found her in that yoga position when she was stressed. And right now, she appeared to be quite repentant. "I am truly sorry for ruining your vacation. Truly."

I shrugged. "Actually, I might as well put you out of your misery and tell you that, well, I've had a job offer. A very good one."

She rolled onto her bum, her eyes stricken. "In California?"

I laughed lightly. "I was on vacation, not job hunting. No, I received a call while I was out there from Jupiter Events. They offered me the director position."

Clara squealed. "Really? Woo-hoo, Greta! Congratulations!"

"I haven't accepted it yet."

"But you will. Right?"

Months ago, the answer to that question was a given. Of course, I would take it. Event planning was all I really knew.

And I was good at it. I'd been devastated to lose that job, especially after all I had learned and the contacts I had made.

But that was before I'd thrown all my orderly ways out the window and hopped a plane to California. Before I met Gus, and Helen, and ... Zac. I knew I had to let them go. My family needed me here. Plus, there was the matter of my past, the many men I'd dated yet never committed to—even when they had.

I glanced at my sister who was sitting up on her haunches, waiting not-so-patiently for my answer. Finally, I said, "Well, I still need to meet with the new owner to officially except the offer and sign the contract"—I took a deep breath—"but, yes, I have decided to accept."

For the second time in one night, Clara let out a whoop so loud I thought I heard the dogs next door start to howl. She sprang up from her position on the floor and nearly knocked me over with a hug around the neck. Whatever misgivings I might have had about my decisions, had disappeared. My wandering was over, and I was home to stay.

Later that night as I lay in bed, sleep elusive, I made a mental list of everything I needed to do the next day. First on the list: Tell Carter that he was free to rent the apartment to someone else.

As Carter and I had discussed previously, when he found another vacation renter to fill out the time I had booked, he would return the remainder of the rent that I prepaid. A win for both of us, really. I turned over onto my side with a sigh, punching my pillow into submission several times.

Still unable to find sleep, I tried counting backwards by twos and then some deep breathing. Sleep would not yet come. I replayed the day's activities, remembering Gram Violet's sweet comment about praying often. A decided sense of peace meandered through my mind and body at the thought of someone actually praying ... for me.

I smiled then, remembering how she had used a letter from long ago as a bookmark. Of all things! She'd said it was her reminder to pray, pray, pray. My eyes lolled, sleep on my doorstep now, my own thoughts turning to nighttime prayers.

*Dear Jesus, please help me to pray more ...*

My eyes shot open. I threw off the covers, swung my legs over the side of the bed, and planted my bare feet on the floor. Grabbing a robe, I hurried over to the bedroom door and flung it open.

"Clara! Get up! We've got some hunting to do!"

# CHAPTER NINETEEN

## ZAC

THE IDEA CAME to me this morning after meeting with the electrician.

"Some of these houses, like yours, need all new wiring. Looks like you've done that. Good on you." He lowered his voice so Gus and Helen couldn't hear him, not that they would've anyway. "But it's especially important to add smart features, you know, for the old folks. I can do it all: voice-activated assistants, fall detection sensors, even smart pill dispensers. All kinds of devices."

"Let's start with the video doorbell and the app for my phone," I told him. "I want to receive an alert if they're ever in trouble."

"Right-o. I'm on it," he said. "You just let me know when you're ready for more, and I'll make sure everything's compatible."

I thanked him and ducked inside to explain to Gus and Helen what kind of work the electrician would be doing.

"Hi, Helen. Is Gus around?"

She looked up from her magazine, frowning. "I can't get him to wake up."

My nerve endings prickled. "You mean he overslept?"

She put down her magazine and shook her head. "He got up as usual and I helped him into his wheelchair"—she shrugged—"but then he fell asleep right in the chair. I had to waste a whole plate of fried eggs!"

I glanced around the room. "Let me check on him. Would that be all right with you?"

"Suit yourself. I wheeled him into the bedroom."

I found Gus sitting upright in his wheelchair, snoring away, his chin resting on his chest. I gave his shoulder a mild shake, hoping for a response. He rallied briefly. I hurried out of the room.

"I'll be right back, Helen. Do me a favor and gather his medications, will you?" I didn't wait for her answer but jogged out the door and upstairs to get my stethoscope and blood pressure cuff.

When I arrived back to their bedroom, Helen was smacking his cheeks lightly with the back of her hand. Gently, I pulled her hand away.

"May I?" I said.

"You're going to examine him?"

"I'd like to listen to his heart. Okay by you?"

Helen nodded, her expression turning serious. She felt for the bed behind her and sat, watching me. I listened to Gus's heart while palpating the radial pulse. It was steady, but a little faint.

I looked at the nightstand and saw all his medicines lined

up. I began to take a mental inventory. Two blood pressure medicines, both with rather high dosages, though they were prescribed to be taken throughout the day.

"Do you know if he took these yet today?"

"He took them all together this morning, otherwise, we both forget. Some of those meds are new and we're not used to them yet."

I let my eyes close as adrenaline seeped right out of me. Far too much blood pressure medicine, in my estimation. And taking it all at one time? Potentially disastrous.

"I'm going to try to help him awaken fully." I took the half glass of water from his nightstand and squatted down beside Gus's wheelchair. "Gus. Can you hear me? It's Zac. Wake up, Gus."

Gus's eyes lolled a bit, and he smacked his lips together. I pushed the glass of water into his hand. "Can you hold this glass for me, buddy?" I knew that if he could hold the glass himself, stroke was doubtful. "Can you take a drink?"

He grunted and managed to take a few sips. Then he handed me the glass, his eyes groggy, but clear. "What're you doing in my bedroom?"

I put my hand on his shoulder, relieved that he was speaking clearly. "Checking on you. Making sure you're all right. Helen here says you fell asleep before eating the breakfast she'd made for you."

He nodded, though still lethargic. "Thank you, son." He put his hand up to rest on mine. "I appreciate it."

"I'd like to get you into bed, Gus, to better maintain your blood pressure," I said. "I'll check it now and then come back in a half hour or so to check it again."

Helen asked, "What happens if it's not okay when you get back?"

"Hopefully it'll be just fine. If not, we might have to take a trip to the hospital." I patted Gus's shoulder again. "But let's start with getting you settled first."

I helped him into the bed and insisted he take another sip of water. Before I left, I asked Helen to make an appointment with Gus's doctor to discuss his medicines. Said I'd be happy to take a call with him as well. I also reminded them both to take their medicines as directed.

As I left their place, I heard Helen tell Gus to hold tight while she whipped him up another breakfast. Outside in the sun, I found myself staring into space. Dr. Perez had suggested that I'd forgotten what it was like to be among the living. And what was it that Greta had said to me about seeing and experiencing? The past few minutes proved her theory. I groaned inwardly, my stubbornness rearing its head again, but not in a condemning way.

It was true. Sometimes examining tissue and writing reports was not enough, neither was hurrying through the hospital, barely seeing the lives I encountered. I had missed out on the small miracles that a simple touch and a careful diagnosis could heal.

Even from miles away, Greta managed to get in my head. I played my last conversation with her over and over in my mind. The more I thought about my behavior the first days she'd arrived—and the months leading up to it—the more I realized that she would have every reason to believe that I'd want to get out from under this house as quickly as possible.

I was a grump. Dissatisfied. And before she showed up, quickly becoming a loner. Deciding to keep Sport was the beginning of healing in that regard, but once Greta entered my world, I knew—there had to be more than my hurt feelings and overall disenchantment with women.

After taking Sport for a romp on the beach, which made me miss that woman more than I thought possible—I brought her back home, and checked on Gus again. Thankfully, his vitals were strong. Helen said he even consumed two helpings of eggs.

Satisfied that Gus was well, I headed back upstairs to my place, grabbed my keys, and headed to the county center to do something I'd thought about while out on the beach earlier. Made a quick stop at in the legal aid office, took their advice, and spent the next hour or so on research.

Satisfied, I printed out what I'd found and drove back home. Instead of a shorter route, I meandered down Olivas Park Drive, cutting through miles of farmland, past stands overflowing with vegetables and fruits, and made a left on the long two-lane road that would take me back to the peninsula that, my idea or not, I now embraced as home.

I pulled up in my driveway, determined to call Greta to see how her grandmother was faring and to find out when she would return. My mood had managed to stay sunny, despite the presence of Carter stepping out of his vehicle.

He watched me exiting my SUV. I didn't know whether to ask him outright why the attention or make a beeline for my front door without a word. Neither seemed all that neighborly. I was working on that, but some annoyances were harder to overcome than others.

"Zac," he said.

I noticed right away that he hadn't addressed me with his usual drippy-voiced *Zachary*.

"Carter," I responded.

"Heard from Greta yet?"

It wasn't any of his business, but I didn't care to lie. He was probably fishing.

"Just ran an errand for her," I said. Though it wasn't a lie, she technically had no idea about my errand. "I'm going to be giving her a call soon."

"That dolt she was engaged to will probably come crawling back now that she's home." He shook his head. "Tell her we all miss her. Kind of liked having her around, know what I mean? What am I saying? Of course, *you* know."

I didn't let on that I had no idea what he was talking about. "I'll pass that along."

"And tell her I put up a new listing for the rental. I should have no problem filling it."

"Filling it?"

"For the rest of her booking, I mean. Should go soon. Probably today." He smacked one hand on top of the other and slid it upward. "Then I'll send that refund right back to her."

I nodded, my mind still trying to grasp the concept that Greta had made a decision not to return. And she'd done it without telling me.

"So you'll tell her for me?" He shot at me in rapid succession with his forefingers. Such a strange dude.

I found my voice. "Yeah. I'll tell her." I turned my back on him then and headed home.

———

I STEWED for hours after running into Carter. Even after all this time, that guy managed to irk me. I sighed heavily, causing Sport to stir. Crawling into bed well beyond my usual time had done nothing to help me sleep it all off. Instead, I lay here, completely awake, thoroughly in knots.

The darkness of the night only served to further heighten my fears.

*That dolt she was engaged to will probably come crawling back now that she's home.*

Pretty Boy had said exactly what I feared the most. What if, when she returned to her grandmother's bedside, the ex was waiting to pounce? He sounded like just the type of guy to take advantage of her vulnerable situation.

And if he did before I had the chance to apologize in person? It would be far too late for us.

# CHAPTER TWENTY

**GRETA**

"GRETA!" Clara was in full whine mode now. She sat rocking on the filthy attic floor, her silk sleep mask stuck to her forehead, and hugging her pillow to her chest.

I was on my feet, digging through a rickety pile of frames and boxes and bric-a-brac. I had more energy than I knew what to do with—and zero interest in putting up with Clara's whining.

I smacked her with an old magazine. Dust flew every-where, and she sneezed like a crusty old man. I handed her a paper towel, and she blew her honker on it.

"We should've cleaned out this attic years ago, Clara."

"Then why not wait one more day?" She sniffled. "C'mon, Greta, this girl needs her sleep!"

"You can sleep when you're dead—isn't that how the saying goes?"

"That's dreadful."

I laughed at her choice of words, which inadvertently reminded me of Carter and his sometimes curious language. That, of course, led me to think about the one person I'd been trying to avoid thinking about all day.

Zac.

I groaned out loud.

"What're you groaning about? I'm the one over here sneezing my guts out when I should be getting my beauty sleep."

"It's nothing. My mind's on hyper speed tonight for some reason. That's all."

Clara eyed me. "Does this have anything to do with the hot boat captain you left in California?"

"He's a doctor."

"Okay. Fine. Dr. Hot Boat Captain."

Even I had to laugh.

"No. Yes ... No!" I bent my knees and picked up another large box. "Stay on topic, would you?"

"I'd rather talk about your love life."

"Why? You working on a new outline?"

"Sorta."

"Then absolutely not." I plunked the box down between us, sending up another plume of dust. "Help me go through this."

Clara sat up, whining the entire time. Sometimes her ability to keep such a successful career going floored me.

I peeked over Clara's shoulder as she opened the box flaps, revealing a mix of trinkets from yesteryear. She plucked something out and held it up. "Look! Here's a photo album I've never seen." She pulled it onto her lap, flipped it open, prying apart its plastic pages. "Here's one of Grams holding you. You're wearing a onesie. And here's another one with Grams. In this one your face is all scrunched up—like you just pooped!"

"Give me that." I reached for the small photo album, vaguely remembering seeing this around when we were little. I flipped through it, many of the pages empty. The photos looked washed out into shades of beige. They were of me, Mom and me, and one was a picture of me being held by a tall man with thinning hair and a happy smile. I lingered on that one like I'd found something private, forbidden. Mom rarely mentioned our father, and I didn't remember that this photo existed. Maybe I never knew.

"I wonder why it was up here with all of Grams's things," Clara said, breaking my concentration. "I mean, you're not some relic."

"You're too little to remember when we moved in here, but I have memories in pieces. I helped Mom bring some of the boxes up to the porch." I closed my eyes, reaching with all my strength for some clarity of that day. "Mom was crying."

"She was?"

I frowned. "Yeah. She was really sad. I didn't understand it all back then, but I probably thought that if I helped her carry in all those boxes, maybe she wouldn't be so sad anymore."

"Wonder why she was sad?"

I slid a look at Clara, my thoughts unspoken.

She nodded, understanding. "Right. Dad had left. That's why we were moving in here, huh."

"As I recall, yes."

"Wow, three new people invaded Grams's little world. No wonder she hid her valuables upstairs."

"Hm."

We were quiet for a minute when suddenly Clara said, "So if you were doing grunt work, hauling boxes in, what was I doing?"

"Nothing. You pretty much laid around on a blanket with your naked cheeks sticking out."

"I did not!"

"You had the worst diaper rash sometimes."

"Stoppppp!"

I laughed lightly. "As I recall, Grams carried you around all day, like the princess you are."

"As it should be."

I placed the photo album back in the box, wiping the dust off the front of it with my hand. The rest of the box contained various supplies, such as blank cards, old postage stamps, and a few probably unusable pens. I closed it up, marked it as reviewed, and carried it over to the other side of the attic, where I put it neatly against the only blank wall.

"See?" Clara said. "This is why you're in the events business. You're organized. If we could marry your organizing skills with my seat-of-the-pants book plotting strategy, imagine the story we could write!"

"One really boring one."

Clara laughed, only it sounded more like a snort. A snorty laugh. She swung one arm open wide, like an announcer. "Okay, folks, what *will* she find in box number two!"

Dutifully, I wiped off the next box, opened it up and pulled out another photo album. Flipped it open to find the photos had faded significantly between the pages of acidic plastic. Again, the few photos were of me, Mom, and the father we barely knew.

The rest of the box was filled with another album or two

and manuals for household items that likely no longer existed, at least in this house.

I glanced over at Clara. "At this rate, we'll be hard pressed to find the treasure that my gut says is in this attic."

"Maybe your gut is actually telling you to take a bath and go to bed."

I ignored her and reached for another photo album from the box. "Look." I showed her an open page.

Clara squealed and grabbed it from my hand. "There *is* one baby photo of me in existence."

I rolled my eyes as she thumbed through the crinkled pages. She sucked in a breath. "Oh, wow," she said. "Here is one of all four of us."

"Really?"

She was right. The album contained one small intact photo of Mom, Clara, me ... and Dad. I zeroed in on his face, trying to remember him, not from this photo, but from real life.

Clara interrupted my thoughts. "Dad looks so angry in that picture, doesn't he?"

I examined him again, hating to admit that she was right. "Maybe he didn't like the cameraman or something."

"I bet the guy was trying to make us all laugh by making kissy noises or something. I can't see any self-respecting father being happy about that." She grinned. "By the way, you and I look great."

"Agreed. The kissy noises worked on us."

"Like a charm!"

I smiled at the silliness of it all, even while, deep down, a growing sense of unrest was tumbling in my belly.

Clara sat back on her bum, hugging her pillow to her

middle again. "I, for one, am happy to see that I wasn't completely forgotten. That album proves that I existed."

Confusion, once again, turned in my stomach, like a long-ago memory that was trying to surface. I began to reach for it in my mind, urging myself to uncover whatever it was that had made me suddenly so ... conflicted.

"Did you hear what I said, Greta?"

I squinted at her, then nodded. "You don't need an old album to prove you existed—your presence proves that."

"Just making sure you were listening. Are we done yet?"

"I don't know, have you found long lost letters from a hundred years ago?"

Clara sighed dramatically. "C'mon, Greta. You really think they're up here? After all this time?"

"Well, this is the one spot you and I have avoided—"

"Like the plague!"

I peeked around the stack of boxes still to comb through. Maybe Clara was right. It was late and there was no promise that we would find what I was looking for—if it even existed. I was driven by a hunch, a strong one, but a hunch just the same.

I poked my fists into my sides and took one last survey of the darkened attic. Box after box after ... wait. I spied something.

I pushed larger boxes aside, sliding them left and right like I was parting the Red Sea to get to a shelving unit on the back wall. One box was particularly heavy. "That's okay, Clara," I mused out loud. "I can move all these heavy boxes myself."

She yawned. "I'm glad for it."

I pushed on, realizing I was on my own. There. On the third shelf up, in the center, was a carved wooden box. Carefully, I pulled it from the shelf and ran my fingers across its intricate lid, which was carved with the shape of a woman dressed in a flapper's costume. Slowly, I lifted the top off the box and ... gasped.

"I hope you didn't see a mouse back there," Clara called, clearly bored with it all.

Slowly, I wagged my head, marveling. Letters. A box full of folded, fragile letters. I wanted to laugh. Or to cry. Either way, I was elated.

"Everything okay over there? Should I make a call to the firehouse? Get some yummy firefighters out here to rescue you?"

"That won't be necessary."

"Aw. Why not?"

"Because I think I have finally found what we've been looking for."

---

WE'D BARELY SLEPT all night, either one of us. Clara and I had organized the letters by date, unable to let even one more hour go by before diving into their glimpse into our great-grandmother's past. I allowed myself a peek at the first couple of letters, but stopped, wanting to savor the rest of them.

Now after a fitful night's sleep, with a second cup of brew poured, Clara and I huddled on the old braided rug, the letters splayed across the coffee table.

"I think we should make copies of all of these," Clara said. "Preserve them forever."

"I wonder if Grams thought the same thing when she shut them up in that beautiful box?"

"It's amazing that she remembered she had."

I sighed and rested my weary self against the couch. "I'm not sure how much she remembers. You know Grams."

"Greta?"

"Hm?"

"I'm really glad you came home, even if under shaky circumstances. Truthfully, Grams does seem to waver in what she remembers."

I nodded. "I'm aware. She asked me last night when I was going to marry Tommy."

"She didn't." Clara pouted. "I guess she forgot, huh?"

"Apparently, but it was worth it to tell her again because she brightened right up. Said, and I quote, 'That guy was all wrong for you, young lady!'"

"She didn't."

"Did."

Clara watched me silently. Then, "Can I ask you about the guy in California now? Zac?"

I took another sip of coffee, my eyes averted. "If you must."

"Your voice changed whenever you mentioned him on the phone. A sister notices these things."

I furrowed my brow. "My voice changed? Like it became deeper? Higher?"

"I'm not joking."

"Neither am I." I shrugged. "Still, I would like to know what you are talking about."

"I think you like him."

"I do like him."

She peered at me, not allowing me to get away with brief answers. "So?"

"What exactly is your question, Clara? When I first met

him, he thought I was the gardener." I didn't mention that, despite his grumpiness, I'd let him kiss me.

"A noble profession."

"That's what I said!"

"But you spent time with him, right?" Clara climbed onto the couch, tucking her legs beneath her. "Lots of time, from what I could tell. And Greta, here we are with all these beautiful letters in our possession and you don't seem happy."

"What makes you think life is about being happy," I shot back.

"Well, I don't think it's about being *unhappy*." She paused. "Do you?"

I didn't look at her. I wasn't unhappy or angry even, just confused. The letters were an amazing find, something I'd never forget and be forever grateful for. But, they were just that —words on paper written long ago by those who have passed on before us.

After I read them all, then what? Life would return to its sameness. Exactly the reason I'd held off finishing them.

I mustered up a smile. "I'll try to do better, kiddo."

Clara shook her head. "Can I be honest?"

"When are you never honest?"

She thought a moment, tapping her chin with her forefinger. "Let me rephrase: Can I give you my opinion?"

When I shrank back, not answering, she added, "Pretty, pretty please?"

"Sure. I guess."

"I've observed something about you."

"Oh, you've observed something."

"Sshh. Sometimes you're really quick to make a decision

about a person, and I think that makes it hard for you to shake that impression."

"Maybe because that impression usually proves to be right."

"Or *maybe* you're afraid to get out of the cycle that you've been on your entire dating life. Guys fall at your feet —it's super annoying to be your sister sometimes. But you always seem to find something wrong with them. Have you ever asked yourself why?"

Tears pushed against my eyes. I mulled this as I had done hundreds of times before in the quiet sanctuary of my mind. I had never spoken my thoughts out loud about this, not even to myself. Until now.

"Because I've always thought that the women in our family had settled rather than chased after love."

"Maybe that's why you always run too."

I turned, looking her straight in the face. "Are you a psychologist now?"

"As a novelist, I have to be. Or at least, psycho."

I let her words sink in, rather than automatically repel me. "The other night, Grams told me she prayed for us all the time."

"I know that she does. I've heard her."

"Did you know that she believes she failed our mom?"

Clara frowned. "Whatever does that mean?"

"I didn't really understand at first, but I think I do now. She was talking about Mom's problem with men, I think."

Clara's eyes lit up. "She doesn't want that to happen to us."

"Right. When I told her she wasn't a failure, she turned it around on me and said that God had turned her foibles—"

"She used that word?" Clara grabbed her phone. "That's

a good one. Hold on while I add it to my notes for a future book."

"May I continue?"

She looked up. "Please do."

"She said God turned her failure into two blessings—us."

"That's so sweet."

"To think, just days ago Grams was on death's door." I looked pointedly at my sister. "And yet, she was able to so clearly make that statement.

"A true miracle." Clara said this with a straight face, though I detected a tinge of contrition.

"Maybe it's time we read the next letter."

"Procrastination. I feel that." She reached across me for the next letter and read it out loud:

DEAREST MOTHER,

WHAT SHALL I EVER DO? I am in the most difficult situation! I was so very wrong to give my heart away and I fear that my mistake will haunt me for a lifetime! Even as I write these words, I am hearing your voice and Daddy's reminding me that all things work together for the good of those who love Christ. I hear the words in my mind's heart, but how can they change what is happening?

There are cruel rumors afoot. The other women have spoken them to each other, and I fear, to the other actors as well. I am afraid that Mr. Winston has done nothing, nothing at all, to chase away the falsehoods that are being told about he and I.

How could a man I loved be so cruel?

Now I am being told I will no longer be needed on set. I am vexed, Mother. Vexed!

LIZZIE

CLARA DROPPED the letter into her lap. "So this confirms it."

"Yes." I glanced at the letter again. "Great-gran did find love—but not with Valentino, apparently."

"Poor Great-gran was ratioed by cancel culture!"

I let out a nervous laugh. "What?"

"That's right. You're not on social media." She sighed in that dramatic way of hers. "Good thing poor Great-gran wasn't either. Sheesh. Ratioed is when a bunch of people gang up on someone on social media—and not in a good way. People can be so mean, am I right?"

"What stuck out to me is her use of the word 'vexed,'" I said. "Now I understand who gave you the drama gene and the vocabulary to go with it."

"Oh, hush, you." Clara reached across me again, accidentally bumping my mouth with her elbow.

"Hey!" I covered the sensitive spot above my top lip with my hand.

"Sorry! I'm so clumsy."

My mind spiraled, the memory vague, not fully attainable, though I believe I'd dreamed of it once. Zac had kissed me on this very spot, and I'd pushed aside a burgeoning memory that was slowly coming into view. As I rubbed the pad of my finger across the light scar that had lingered since childhood, I was taken back—to the day we first moved into this house.

"Greta? Is something wrong? Did that really hurt you?"

I gave my sister a guarded look. There was a fourth person here that day we had all moved in. I was suddenly sure of it. How could a memory appear when it had to have been there all along, underneath the surface of my consciousness?

A hot flash of stress came over me as I avoided looking at my beautiful, overly dramatic, introverted sister. "Clara," I finally said, "I need you to hear me out."

"That doesn't sound good."

"It depends on your perspective, I guess." I shifted toward her, conjuring up my nerve. "Remember when we were talking about that day that we all moved in here?"

"When I officially became royalty? That day?"

"Well, yes. Honey, I remembered something just now." My fingers found that scar on my face again, and I rubbed it like it was a good luck charm. "I'd been running back and forth between the moving truck and the house. Grams kept warning me not to run. There used to be a dozen rosebushes out in front of the house, and she was worried we'd get hurt by the thorns—do you remember?"

She shook her head, no.

"Right. You were a baby. But I kept running up the path, even when I couldn't see in front of me whenever Dalton handed me another box."

"Dalton?"

"One time, I dropped off a box on the porch, then I spun around and ran right down between those two lines of rose bushes. When I got to the moving truck, I hid underneath it. I think I was just being a kid, playing a game, you know?" I inhaled, gathering courage. "That's when I overheard something I don't think I was ever meant to hear."

"And you remember it now?"

"I think so. Since I'd been hiding, Dalton didn't see me coming and tossed one of the boxes out to the curb just as I popped out. It hit me right here"—I tapped my scar—"on my lip."

"So that's how you got that scar, though honestly, I hardly ever notice it."

"I had forgotten what happened, how that box hit me, and how I'd fled in tears to our grandmother."

Clara turned quiet a moment. "This house holds all kinds of memories, doesn't it?"

"Some it is still revealing."

Clara eyed me. "You never did tell me who Dalton was, though. A relative?"

"Uh-huh." I could barely meet her gaze. "At least, I think so."

"On Mom or our father's side?"

I raised my gaze to meet hers. "On your side."

# CHAPTER TWENTY-ONE

**Greta**

**One Week Later**

When I was young, my mom would say to appreciate every moment because you'll never get it back. Our grandmother also opined about the speed in which time flew by, stealing with it pieces of our lives that we want to hold onto.

This past week flew by like that: a stiff summer breeze that could not be stopped. When that memory from moving day presented itself like an unopened clam shell, I wasn't certain whether it would produce a pearl or a grain of insignificant sand.

It remained to be seen what Clara would determine it to be, a journey for my sister to take, should she decide to, in her own time.

With the help of Gram's intermittent recollections, I was

able to piece together the memories that I had carried with me for so long. My mother's tears, all those years ago, were the only ones I remembered her shedding about the move, and Dalton's face, still a watery memory.

When my mom married my father, Grams told us, she was already pregnant—with me. My parents separated for a time, and she fell again for a man who would break her heart. With a little coaxing, I learned that my father had tried, but ultimately, refused to raise another man's child. He chose to leave all of us behind. Somehow, I think I knew that part all along.

Dalton's appearance that day was the only time I saw him in our midst. If it weren't for the little scar that I carried with me, I might not have ever remembered that he had once existed—and certainly may be somewhere out there still.

Thankfully, the knowledge that Clara and I were likely half-siblings had done nothing to tear us apart. Quite the opposite. Our mom and grandmother had sacrificed to keep us together under the same roof, to love us unconditionally, and to keep us blissfully ignorant of how our little family came to be.

The house bustled with a warm wind now, the screen door allowing that breeze to whip right through our home. Clara and I finally read the letter in our great-gran's box with the latest date and, as it turned out, it was not written by her at all, but by the "infamous" 'R.'

I smoothed the paper between my thumb and forefinger, wishing to go back in time and sit at Great-grandmother Elizabeth's feet. Maybe then we could learn the details of how truly heroic our great-grandfather Henry had been. That, unfortunately, was a detail about her mother's life that our Grams did not recall.

Until heaven, this would have to suffice:

DEAREST ELIZABETH,

I AM WRITING to you again, for solace and comfort. My heart is in tatters. I fear my life will never be the same. How could it be? I loved him, you know. Deeply. And yet, he did not return my affections.

Of course, you knew this. You saw it from afar. You tried to warn me, but I would not listen. This is how I know you to be a true friend. My one, true confidante.

I suppose you now know the fate of your former suitor too. Mr. Winston married Rachel, who was with child. Not too many days passed by before he left his young wife and their baby. Imagine! I grieve for her, though I was none too pleased to learn she had spent time alone with him, knowing full well how your heart was involved with his.

Oh, if only I had the ability and the strength, like you, to foresee a future filled with heartache and to choose not to step further into the abyss.

How did you do it? Was it your prayers, Lizzie? Your Mother and Father's prayers too? Ah, but the Almighty had one more trick up his sleeve, did he not? Who else could bring a sweet, gentle soul like your Henry all the way to California to rescue you from certain spinsterhood? Why, he came in like a swashbuckler on the silver screen!

I must go now. I covet your prayers for my broken heart.

FONDLY,

Anna-Rose

I PUT THE LETTER DOWN, my heart aching for Anna-Rose, aka "R," all these years later. Did my grandmother pray for her? Did the woman's heart mend? Something told me she did and it did. I had to believe that for my sanity's sake.

———

CLARA WANDERED into the living room where I sat on the couch, my packed suitcase on the floor next to me. "May I read it again?"

I grinned and handed her the envelope that I'd received in the mail, a crisp new postage stamp affixed to the outside.

She bit her bottom lip and squealed a little, like she'd just been handed Willy Wonka's golden ticket.

I watched as my sister re-read the penned words that had found their way deep into my heart at a time when I needed them most. She hummed an acknowledgment as she read.

Clara dropped her hand to her lap, visibly swooning. "May I have a copy? You know, for inspiration?"

I laughed at this. She'd just paid the letter's author the ultimate compliment. "I promise to send you one."

My sister continued to wear that dreamy smile of hers, the kind I'd seen a time or two whenever she had wrestled her way through a tough love scene. At this moment, my heart's desire turned to her, a hope and a prayer for her future because, frankly, being her muse was becoming ... exhausting.

I laughed aloud before I could catch myself.

"What's that about?" she asked.

I shrugged. "Just thinking."

"I've been thinking, too."

"About?"

"What if sometimes heroism doesn't ride in on a white horse, but on a postage stamp?" she said.

I laughed harder now. "Aren't you going to write that down for your next book?"

"Nah. It's a freebie. I'm giving it to you."

We laughed until we were both sniffling from tears. When we'd quieted some, Clara said, "I've been thinking about something else, too."

"Sounds dangerous."

"Remember when we were kids and Grams told stories of how Great-gran loved to put on plays at the town theater?"

I nodded. "I do remember that. Just like I remember Grams and Mom singing silly songs that sounded like something straight out of Vaudeville."

Clara tossed her head back and laughed. "They were ridiculous."

"Yes." I smiled, widely. "I remember."

"Sad that she never realized her dream of becoming a famous actress of the silver screen."

"Oh, I don't know. It sounds like she took the things she learned, the good *and* the bad, and made a new one instead."

After a moment of quiet between us, Clara said, "What do you want to do with this?" She held up the engagement photo Tommy had sent, the one meant to fool me into running back to him.

"Give it away to someone who wants it?"

She stood up, walked over to the garbage can, and

dropped it in. "Done." She dusted off her hands by smacking her palms together and joined me on the couch.

"You know I'll check in on you and Grams often," I said.

"I know, but don't you worry about us."

"Hm. I'll try not to."

Clara smiled. "So. Tell me how your call with Jupiter Events went."

"They understood."

"That you're gettin' out of Dodge, flying the coup, packin' it in."

"All those clichés and more. I just hope ..."

"What? That you've made the right decision?"

I nodded. For my entire childhood, I'd believed that, despite the nigglings of questions beneath the surface, everything was okay. It was, for the most part, except that our mom carried the burden of a secret. Worse, I carried it too. Now that the lore of my own life had been replaced with reality, that burden had lifted.

"Don't be," Clara said. "You must be willing to let go of the life you've planned to have to grab the life that is waiting for you."

Tears overcame me, as I thought of how those words could be applied to my great-gran's life too.

Clara reached out. "I stole that quote from the author Joseph Campbell, but it applies, Greta. Someday, maybe I will apply it to my life too."

We sat in silence, Clara and I. Our lives might look quite different in the near future. I didn't want to run away anymore, I wanted to run *to* whatever life I was destined to have. Somehow, I thought Mom would approve.

My phone buzzed. "My ride's here." I stood.

"Time to go?" Clara asked.

I nodded, a second rush of tears in my throat. Clara came over, hugged me tightly, then pulled back, her hands holding mine. "Get out of here."

"Okay." Though my career wore a big question mark on its head, I knew that I needed to go back to California. When I checked the vacation rental website, I was surprised to see that my little apartment in Carter's home was still open. I'd rebooked it in a hurry, never stopping to consider what I would say when I arrived.

I headed out the front screen door and onto the porch when Clara stopped me. "Oh, and Greta?" she said.

"Yes?"

"If I call you to come rushing back ... just say no."

I laughed lightly at this and blew her a kiss before stepping off the porch.

I used to hear my mom and my grandmother wax poetic about our great-gran's days in Hollywood by the Sea and I would think: Why didn't she stay instead of going home and settling for an existence devoid of true love? But now I understood: Great-grandmother Elizabeth never settled at all.

She married her hero—and never looked back.

# CHAPTER TWENTY-TWO

**ZAC**

I HELD out hope that I would see Greta again. I'd prayed for her to return, a hope against hope that she would. "Maybe you should ride out to Indiana on your white steed and proclaim your love for her," Carter had announced one day, when I'd approached him for help.

Then he cackled like a seabird choking on a French fry.

I had considered it many times. Rolled it around in my brain and even allowed my finger to hover over the computer keyboard while I looked for a flight. But I always came back to what she had said when she left: *I'm not ready.*

In the end, I made some decisions, took care of some things I felt compelled to do, and put my trust in God to bring her back. Because when she returned, I wanted her to be ready. For me. For us. For a future that I had yet to define. All I knew was that both she and I would be in it.

Preferably without Carter anywhere nearby.

Although ... Carter and I had made a truce of sorts. He had cut ties with Lisa and further sealed our truce when he spilled it that Greta had, indeed, decided to come back.

"What time is she getting here?" Helen asked.

"From what I hear, in an hour." I took another sip of coffee—horrible burnt coffee that Helen had made hours ago.

"More hash browns?" She held the pan of greasy potatoes in front of her, expectantly.

I patted my belly. "No, thank you, Helen. I'm quite full."

Gus held up his fork. "I'll have more of what you're serving up, Missus."

She promptly slid the whole shiny mess onto his plate and then tossed the pan into the sink.

I had shown up this morning, not to hang a shelf or meet a contractor, but to share a meal with this couple who had become like family to me. In the past couple of months, they had made me laugh again—despite myself. Greta's part in that wasn't lost on me.

"Well, if you boys don't need my cooking skills anymore," Helen said, "I think I'll go and get myself looking presentable."

"Aw, you look fine, Helen," Gus said. "Just perfect."

"Liar!" She gave him a smooch on his nearly bald head and disappeared.

Gus looked at me deadpan. "She's got it bad for me."

I chuckled, swigged the last of my coffee and stood. "It was a pleasure having breakfast with you sir."

"Don't *sir* me. We're friends here, you and me. Not buyer and seller, not tenant and landlord, but friends." He paused. "Scratch that—we're family!"

I stuck out my hand. "That we are."

"So you'll bring her around when she gets here?"

I wanted to tell him that there might be a delay, that I sorely needed some time alone with her, to see where she stood. It was said that pathologists were experts in predicting. Though that was true, I could not predict why Greta had chosen to return, or if it had anything at all to do with me.

But I held out hope.

I hadn't realized until now that the women I'd dated in the past had done the heavy lifting, while I followed along, thinking I was doing right by them. I was with them in my head, but not where it mattered—the heart. Greta changed all that. I was no longer ambivalent—I knew that I wanted her, without a doubt.

"If she'll have me," I said.

He pointed a stubby finger at me. "Don't worry, son. She will."

"How do you know that?"

"She's not an idiot." But he looked at me as if I might very well be one myself.

## Greta

THE DRIVER DROPPED me off in front of Mermaid Manor, that tattered flag still flapping its welcome to weary travelers. My heart surged with hopefulness this time, instead of apprehension. I found myself lingering outside, standing in anticipation of what may come while reveling in the soft breeze on my skin. Even evidence of new weeds poking through the ground made me smile.

Well, a little.

I glanced over to Zac's driveway. Empty. I wondered where he'd gone and immediately chastised myself. When I'd told him I wasn't ready, I meant it. Despite the letter he'd written saying he missed me, what right did I have to wish I knew where he was now and what he might be doing?

"Oh, it's Greta!"

I spun around at the sound of dear Helen's voice.

She approached me with her chubby arms raised for a hug. "Come here and let me look at you!"

I folded myself in her embrace, laughing as I did. "It's only been a few weeks, Helen."

"Aw, but they were long weeks, let me tell you, young lady." Her eyes glimmered. "Old Gus and I have missed you around here." Her gaze drifted to Zac's front door before swinging back to meet mine.

"I've missed you too." I pressed my lips together, searching her face for signs of stress. "You said on the phone that you and Gus needed me here, that you had something very personal to discuss with me. Is everything okay, Helen?"

Helen spied my suitcase. "You haven't even unpacked yet!"

"There'll be plenty of time for that later," I said with a shrug.

"Well, come on in, then. Gus'll be so happy to see you!"

I followed her, passing an upgraded doorbell as I did. Inside, the shades were open with afternoon sunlight pouring in. I almost did a double take, as the house smelled like an Italian restaurant, with nothing burning.

"Gus!" Helen hollered down the hall to him.

"Hold your horses!" he hollered back.

Helen gave me a mock roll of her eyes. "He wasn't doing too good this week, but Zac fixed him right up."

"Zac?"

"The dear man charged right into the bedroom. Said he thinks Gus is taking too much blood pressure medicine. He's already talked to Gus's doctor on the phone, and he changed his meds." She shook her head, like she couldn't believe their luck. "That boy has been such a blessing to us."

I tried to keep my reaction neutral because, to me, Zac was much more than a boy. Much more.

Gus emerged from the bedroom looking weary but happy. "Well, there's a sight for sore eyes if I've ever seen one."

"Hello, Gus." I leaned down to give him a hug. "How're you doing?"

"Never better." He smiled.

"Go on and sit, Greta," Helen said.

Silence lofted into the room like a blanket from heaven: cozy, comfortable, and full of questions. "Helen told me of your blood pressure troubles, Gus."

Gus frowned. "Now why'd you have to go and bother her about all that?"

"She asked!"

I watched them volley for a while, hiding my laughter, yet secretly enjoying every minute of them. To the outside world, they were sparring, but I'd learned this was another way these old birds loved each other.

"Greta doesn't want to hear you bickering with me anymore, Helen," Gus was saying.

Helen waved at him. "Oh, go on."

I smiled at them, bemused. "Since I'm here, would you like to tell me something?"

They exchanged a glance, while Helen, hands clasped, nervously pressed her thumbs together again and again.

Gus spoke up. "We heard a rumor that you think Zac had it out for us."

I frowned.

"That dippy ex-girlfriend of his was out on the driveway last week, wearing a pantsuit and talking loudly into her phone like she was the Queen of England!"

I tried to picture Queen Elizabeth... standing outside on a cell phone ... wearing a pantsuit ...

"Bottom line, young lady, is that Zac saved me." Gus wiped his brow with a napkin, slowly, and lowered his voice. "It is not easy to admit when you've been had. I made a bad investment—

"Thanks to that Carter," Helen cut in.

"It was on me, Helen." Gus's eyes flashed, the most fire I'd ever seen from him. "Both Carter and I made bad decisions, and it cost us. You've been inside that place, Greta, so I'm sure you know the house is hurtin' some. Trust me, that boy's having to work overtime to keep food in his mouth."

"I am so sorry to hear this," I said, my heart twisting at their predicament.

Helen pouted, looking at her husband. "Now you're makin' me feel bad."

"All I'm saying is we were blessed to have someone like Zac buy our place." Gus's voice shook. "Kept a roof over our heads, and not just any roof—the one we've been livin' in for forty years."

"Is this why Zac's not exactly a fan of Carter's?"

Helen slapped her knee. "Ha! Not a fan. That's one way to put it."

I continued, "Lisa mentioned that you had experienced some financial trouble, but I considered it rumor."

"Never listen to a woman dressed in gold, carrying a shovel." Helen shook a finger at me. "That's what I always say."

"It's true," Gus said. "She does say that."

Helen calmed some and looked at me, forcefully. "Greta, we wanted to tell you all this ourselves because, well, we watch the Hallmark Channel"—she looked at Gus—"don't we Gus?"

"I plead the fifth on that one!"

I suppressed a laugh.

"Anyway," Helen said, "it always seems like some kind of lie keeps the people in those movies from becoming a couple. We just didn't want to be the ones stopping you."

I couldn't help the laughter that came rolling out of me. "You two are the sweetest people." Despite all the sad news they confirmed, I found myself smiling at their motivation. No matter what my future held, I would not forget these two as long as I lived.

"You must be exhausted," Helen finally said.

I stood and reached for the handle of my suitcase, leaning on it. "I am a little tired. I think I'll go up to the apartment now." I was nearly out the door when I stopped and spun back around. "I'm so glad to be back."

Gus nodded. "And we're happy you're here too, Greta."

I was halfway across the divide between the two houses when a husky, familiar voice broke the silence. "Greta." I stopped, my heart thudding in my chest and sending heat ricocheting through me.

"Zac."

"You've returned."

"I'm back." At that moment, I wanted to say *for good* but instead, "Well, for the rest of the summer."

I watched his face considering me until an agreeable awkwardness stood between us, the kind that was full of what ifs. Only instead of asking myself what if I were to leave, I desperately wanted to ask, *What if I were to stay?*

"So you found each other." We both turned at Carter's voice. I hadn't noticed that his car was back in his driveway, and given what I had learned from Gus and Helen, I wasn't sure whether to feel pity or anger.

"Hello, Carter."

He leaned against the side of it, one hand in the pocket of light tan slacks, his hair gelled to perfection, and those mirrored glasses firmly in place. He could double as a movie star, and I'm sure that's what he was going for. Pity was winning out.

"Good to see you again, Greta," he said.

"You too, Carter." I stayed impersonal. "I think there's something wrong with the rental portal because my payment didn't go through. I can write you a check tonight."

He shifted, almost nervously, his body language no longer looking quite as confident as before. I reached for my purse. "Or I could do it right now if you—"

"No!" Carter gestured with a wave of his arm then appeared to make eye contact with Zac before changing course. "I think you'd better talk to your boyfriend about that." He got into his Mercedes, backed out of the driveway, and sped off.

I glanced at Zac. "He's so very ..."

"Strange?"

For some reason, his finishing my thought caused me to burst out laughing. I was suddenly all of sixteen and it felt ... great.

He cleared his throat, looking so very serious now. "There's no balance due on the apartment."

"I don't understand. He could have booked the next month easily, I think. Why would he ..." My words drifted off, watching emotion flicker across Zac's face. He looked determined, slightly flustered, and downright sexy all rolled into one man.

I continued. "I mean, he gave me a refund."

"Because I booked the rest of the summer."

I paused, letting that sink in. Zac actually paid money to Carter. "For me?"

A tickle of a smile emerged on his face. "Maybe."

"Oh, I get it. You didn't want him to book some rowdy crowd in there that would be keeping you up all night."

Zac groaned. "Now I sound like a real jerk."

I tapped my chin, thinking. "Unless there was some other reason for you to pay off the neighbor?"

He let out a low growl now, and wrapped his arm around my waist, cinching me close.

I was undeterred. "Because, why would a jerk give his hard-earned money to his biggest nemesis if it weren't for a really great reason?"

He quirked a smile. "Why indeed?"

I laughed. "Whatever reason would he have?"

His strong arms continued to hold me. "A beautiful woman who's got me wrapped around her pinky."

I tilted my chin up further still. "I could see that."

He leaned toward me now and brushed my lips with a kiss. "Worth every penny."

Though I had been reveling in our banter, my mind raced at his kindness ... and his touch. When had anyone ever done such a thing for me, especially knowing I might not ever return? It was ... unbelievable to me.

And yet wholly true.

A glimpse of him told me he, too, had turned serious. I began to speak, to thank him properly, when he blurted out, "I owe you an apology."

I lifted my chin, narrowing my eyes slightly, knowing what I had to do. "No, you really don't. I'm the one who wasn't fully honest with you, Zac. I know that now."

"Greta, no." He shook his head vehemently, his eyes holding regret. "Here's something you need to know: I haven't been on vacation."

I tilted my head now, confused as ever. "Wait. What?"

"Sabbatical. A forced one." He blew out a harsh breath, eying me, as if looking for a sign of rejection. "You were right. Everything you said was right. I'm an intense guy, but that's no excuse for ignoring the people closest to me."

I shushed him, reached up and hugged him around the neck. "It's okay, Zac."

He buried his face in my hair, whispering, "You're too good for me."

I pulled back a little and shook my head. "I'm sorry about the sabbatical, but I'm glad that you chose to spend some of it with me."

"Best sabbatical I've ever had."

I laughed lightly at this, knowing I still had some owning up to do myself. "You were right, you know, about me. I did exactly what you said—lied by omission."

His eyes narrowed, looking pained. "I never said that."

"You implied it." I sighed. "And you were right on. It was

a lot easier to be the victim in my scenario, to put the blame somewhere else rather than face my own mistakes. I should never have accepted Tommy's proposal. Nor should I have allowed my other relationships to reach that point."

"Wait. You had *other* proposals?"

I snapped a look at him. "Two."

"Wow."

I raised both palms, trying to explain. "I knew they were coming, and I should have headed them off before they happened." I pressed a hand to my face, wishing not to relive all that. "I didn't accept them. I promise."

"I meant, Wow, you're popular."

I laughed, nearly giddy that he was standing in front of me, mercy written all over his face.

"Forgive me?" I said.

He stroked the side of my face, sending a tiny chill down my side. "Absolutely," he whispered. "I hope you'll forgive me too."

"Of course, I do, Zac."

We stood there, his warm hand cupping my face, staring into each other's eyes. Slowly, he stepped back. "I got you something." He said it casually, as if he'd been at the store picking up a carton of milk and had plucked something from the candy aisle. He pulled several folded sheets of paper from the back pocket of his jeans. "Here."

I reached for the pages and gave him a quirk of a smile. "A list of addresses?"

"Houses."

"You hate looking at real estate."

"But you don't."

I smiled. "So, you were carrying these around with you?"

He squirmed slightly, in that cool nerdy way of his, and

another thrill shot right through me. "I picked this list up for you several weeks ago, in hopes ..."

"In hopes?"

He swallowed back his reply, his Adam's apple shifting. His face awash with fresh emotion. "That you'd come home."

I took in his handsome face, a hint of fresh tears welling up inside of me. He'd called this place, far away from the only family I'd ever known, home. "Is that why you wrote me a love letter?"

He startled, his skin turning pink, then slowly deepening. "You received my letter?"

I smiled.

"I thought that, perhaps, it had not reached you yet."

"It did," I said. "Zac, I don't know what to say."

He watched me with a pained expression. "I wasn't trying to manipulate you. You said you weren't ready, and I have to accept that."

"Zachary Holt, that letter was the most touching, romantic thing I have ever received in my entire life. I will cherish it always."

His lips parted as he assessed me, awareness showing in his expression. Though we were outside for the world to see, and I had been traveling for many hours, I wanted to ditch the pretense and melt right into him. Instead, I turned my attention to the gift he had handed me. I unfolded the pages, a printout of addresses and names. I glanced up at him, then, questioning.

"It's every house along this part of the coast that was here in the twenties and thirties. Well, the ones that are still standing. Thought it might interest you."

My heart leaped. "It's like a ... treasure map."

He laughed, his voice deep, hearty.

My mind began to percolate with business ideas, starting with, perhaps, a charity event—a fundraiser of some kind—that included a tour of historic homes. Confidence rose within me.

"When I paid that parking ticket a few weeks ago, I noticed there was a legal aid center at the county building. They helped me research that list for you," he said. "Maybe you'll find what you've been looking for."

My eyes took in his face, the curious, kind eyes, the morning stubble. His mouth. *I believe I already have.*

"Oh, Greta," he whispered, reaching out and pulling me close.

He said my name with such force, such meaning, that I nearly cried from the ache in it. "I've missed you terribly," I told him.

"That's what I was hoping for." He leaned back, tipping my chin up with his fingers. "Tell me why you really came back."

"Because I was tired of running."

"What about the job?"

"I turned it down."

He exhaled, and it sounded like relief. "Tell me you're here to stay."

My breath caught in my throat. "If you'll have me."

Zac kept my gaze, releasing another deep sigh. "I was wrong that night, in your apartment," he said, "when I asked you to stay."

"Oh."

"I told you I wanted to find out where it may lead, but that's not true anymore." His eyes lit with resolve, fire.

"Greta, I've known you a month—nearly two if you count those cruel days and weeks when you left me—"

"I didn't exactly leave you, Zac."

"Not having you here felt like a gut punch. I hated it."

I couldn't stop staring at him, leaning in to every word he said.

He looked down a moment, as if to gather his thoughts, then raised his chin. A tangible current traveled between us, like an electric shock. "I meant everything I said in that letter I wrote to you, Greta. I don't need more time. I already know where this has led—I want you here forever. With me."

# CHAPTER TWENTY-THREE

**GRETA**

ONE MONTH Later

FOR AS LONG AS I could remember, I wanted the life of a romance novel heroine. While Clara only wrote about romance, I had pursued it, largely in the wrong way and *always* with the wrong man—just like Mom.

The thing about burdens that are passed from generation to generation was they could be stopped. Grams lamented what had happened to her daughter, my mom, and how she believed she had failed her. But I could never place that kind of blame on someone else, and neither would our mom, who, as her life on earth came to a close, renewed her long-dormant faith in the Lord.

Hard things happened in life, despite our best efforts to avoid them, but through faith, God could take even our worst failures and make them into something beautiful. My family, past and present, was a picture of that.

Still, I longed to see the broken part of our family's chain repaired, once and for all.

"Ready?" Zac's voice eased into my thoughts. I looked over to where he had appeared at the top of the steps. I'd been sitting out here on the deck, waiting for him.

He took my hand as we descended the stairs, fingers of sunlight still shooting across the sky. The time was encroaching on eight o'clock.

Sport met us at the bottom of the stairs. Zac unhooked her leash from a post as Sport danced all around me. I bent down to pet her, and she leaped into my arms and slobbered on my chin.

"Greta?"

I put Sport down and tilted a look up at him. "Yes?"

Zac frowned, gesturing at the planter beds in front of his house. "Did you pull the weeds?"

I covered my mouth and straightened, then raised both hands in a shrug. "Guilty."

Zac smiled, then roared. His arm came around my neck and hooked me close. He kissed my temple. "I'll hire a gardener tomorrow."

I shoved him gently. "You will not. Let me."

His eyes reflected the setting sun. "Okay, but don't take guff from the neighbors, especially any tough guys."

I rose up on my tiptoes and kissed his cheek. "Yes, Doctor."

He held my hand and we walked out to the sand, the horizon in view as the sun made its descent. I slipped out of my sandals, and hung them from my fingers, reveling in the soft friction of sand in each step. Sport stayed close, as if wanting to be part of the *us* that had bonded even more so in the past few weeks.

"Stop."

I quirked a questioning look at Zac. His sunglasses did little to hide the mischievous smile forming. We were in a wide part of the beach. He pulled me in front of him, wrapping an arm around me, and pointed to the horizon with the other.

"Keep your gaze straight ahead," he said, his mouth warm against my ear. "We're looking for a legend, you and I."

I caught my tongue between my teeth, feeling the anticipation rising. We'd learned this breezy beach had seen its share of legends, and now it was our turn.

"Here it goes," he whispered in that husky way of his. "Keep watching. Don't blink."

I giggled.

"Ssshh."

I kept my eyes focused ahead but couldn't clear the smile from my face.

"Three ... two ... one." The timbre of his voice rose slightly. "And ... there!"

I gasped. No way. We'd seen it! The legendary green flash ... and it was gorgeous. I spun around to find Zac grinning at me. He held a lush green box out to me.

"Open it," he said.

Emotion caught in my throat. I flipped a look into his eyes. I had not seen this coming and wanted to lean into it all, capture every nuance of the moment—I had a feeling I would be telling this story for years to come.

"Well?"

I took the box from him, opened it, and gasped. The ring

sparkled like a star. I immediately slipped it onto my finger, wanting to protect his gift to me.

Zac took my hand then and dropped to the sand, Sport leaping back and forth over his calves, until I began to laugh. "I'm trying to have a serious moment here," he said.

"I know!" My voice rose to the oddest, silliest pitch. I laughed again and took his precious face in my hands now. Oh, how I loved this man.

"Greta," Zac said, sobering some, "legend has it that in matters of the heart, once you've seen that green flash out there on the horizon, you can never go wrong."

*Oh, my.*

"But I don't need a legend to tell me something that I can see with my own eyes and feel with my own heart. I love you, Greta. I knew it that first day. I was a hothead, but you were kind and bold, and each day after that all I wanted to do was know you more. I still do and always will."

My laughter turned to tears, the happy, drippy kind. I dropped to my knees in the sand, facing him. In his eyes, I saw unabashed love, the kind that wouldn't quit when the gleam of life dulled some. "I love you back."

"Marry me?"

Sport jumped into the mix, leaping and bucking, her bark sounding like a croon of *I love yous* all around us.

"Yes," I said, my voice a quivering mess. "I can't wait to marry you, Zac. You're my forever and I love you madly."

And though the sun had sunk beneath the horizon, its fiery afterglow lit our path home.

## ACKNOWLEDGMENTS

Many thanks to my family for your constant inspiration: Dan, Matt, Angie, and Emma; and my parents, Dan and Elaine Navarro. I love you all.

Thanks also to Jennifer Crosswhite for editing this novel, and for putting up with my late night brainstorming emails.

And a big thank you to my readers for taking a chance on this story. I hope you loved it!

# ABOUT THE AUTHOR

JULIE CAROBINI writes inspirational beach romances. Her father is the author of *Navarro's Silent Film Guide* and shared his love of the silver screen with Julie and her brothers when they were kids. *Chasing Valentino* is a nod to those years. Julie is the author of 20+ novels across two names, and has won awards from both ACFW and NLAPW. She lives near the beach in California with her husband, Dan, and loves spending time with their three grown kids.

Pick up a free story for your e-reader here:
**www.juliecarobini.com/free-book**

Made in the USA
Columbia, SC
17 May 2023

16866735R00169